Sgt. Janus

SPIRIT-BREAKER

SGT. JANUS, SPIRIT-BREAKER
©2020 Jim Beard

A Flinch Books Production
Flinch Books and the Flinch Books logo
© Jim Beard and John C. Bruening
www.facebook.com/flinchbooks

Expanded Edition

Previous edition published by Airship 27 Productions in 2013

Cover illustration and design by Jeffery Ray Hayes
PlasmaFire Graphics, LLC
www.plasmafiregraphics.com

Interior layout and formatting by Maggie Ryel

ISBN: 978-0-9977903-4-4

For the Little Woman, who is always with me in spirit.
Jim Beard

TABLE OF CONTENTS

"It is well-known and stringently documented that children and animals possess a high degree of sensitivity to the Unknown. I first encountered a spirit at the tender age of eight years old when a tutor of mine – my parents insisted on private schooling, though I would have preferred to be among more of my youthful peers – sat me down one fine day and explained to me in no uncertain terms that he was deceased and had been for at least twenty years.

"An event such as that is bound to either break a person or set them on a path to their destiny."

Excerpted from "Janus Speaks!"
The Mount Airy Eagle
April 10 Edition

Chapter I

THE PORTOBELLO CETACEAN

How strange. The very moment my pen touched the paper to write, a dream I had several nights ago came rushing back in on me like flood waters. In it, I stood in front of a cave somewhere, quite unclothed yet all together comfortable. I knew not the location of the cave, but was unconcerned by this. Suddenly, a man stood before me, as naked as myself, and I asked him what was it he had come to tell me. His identity was unclear, though I felt I should know him.

Then, a…substance began to come out of me. Through my mouth, my nose, my ears, the corners of my eyes, and…other places. It felt cold; I remember very well the shocking coldness of it. Grey and clammy, it reminded me of the tentacles of a squid or perhaps even the undulating body of an eel. The man before me only stared, seemingly unsurprised by the extrusion of this substance, but then opened his mouth wide, as if to scream. For my own part, I could only stand there and observe its slowly growing state, until, finally, it blackened my vision and I awoke, unsure of the dream's ultimate ending and curious as to its deeper meaning.

I sincerely hope that the dream has nothing whatsoever to do with my recent ordeal.

I have been asked to put pen to paper as a record of the events of 4 May. It is a rather odd request, yet I must admit that doing so may help me sort through those events and put them in order in my own mind. As it stands, my experiences in the presence of my benefactor remain with me to this day and, at the moment, I can regrettably make little sense of them.

I have also been directed to omit no detail, no matter how small or seemingly insignificant, in my accounting.

I feel as if I must stress, here at the beginning of this record, that new experiences are not anathema to me and I openly welcome the pursuit and gainful massing of knowledge. There are many things we do not know of in our mortal lives and, given the short time we are accorded on Earth, it is our duty, I feel, to learn all that we can. That said, before my journey I humbly acknowledged my ignorance and naiveté of the supernatural world; yet now I feel as if I have brushed against that world and know something of it.

In April of this year I had cause to seek help on a matter not lightly spoken of to strangers – or, for that matter, perhaps even to loved ones. Events unfolded that vexed me to an extent that I sought professional aid, someone whose knowledge base would bring light into a very dark shadow that had befallen me in my home, my very life. Asking about, surreptitiously and somewhat timidly, I'm afraid, I was recommended to approach one Sgt. Janus of Mount Airy.

I had not previously heard of the man, or in actuality his supposed profession. What was I to think of a personage who claimed, or so I was told, to ease the suffering of those afflicted with the supernatural? After a week's deliberation and after much internal struggle, I made my way to Sgt. Janus and, hopefully, a cessation of my troubles.

The trip to Mount Airy was, in itself, uneventful. The little town was unfamiliar to me but only a bit over two hours' journey by motorcar and I made good time. Early May was breezy and warm and the countryside picturesque and inviting; there was little hint of what awaited me in short order. Mount Airy is something of a misnomer, as the town rests nowhere near a mountain – or any substantial hill for that matter – but when I had reached its boundaries I found it to be a place seemingly untouched by time. Small farms on its outskirts gave way to tiny tumble-down cottages and a smattering of hovels – all of which spoke of a simple people with simple pursuits. Saying this, I spied absolutely no such people as I drove past their homes on my way to the center of the tiny village.

Presently, I came to a small, somewhat dilapidated service station. Pulling into the station I detected movement in the small building's sole doorway and soon found an old, wizened man in suspenders and half-moons ambling up to my vehicle. I made sure to affix my face with my best smile and, having braked, I shut off the motor.

"Good day," he said without a smile of his own. "Wha' can I do for you, miss?"

Assuming there was to be no pleasantries exchanged with this man, I came to the point and told him that I was a stranger to these parts and sought the dwelling of Sgt. Janus. His demeanor noticeably cooled by several degrees, if that was possible, and he frowned at me.

"Aye, I can see that you may be in need of his services," he croaked. "I can give you directions, and may the Lord watch over you."

Though the ride into Mount Airy was not altogether unpleasant and I am always glad to discover new places on the map, the frustrations of my overall situation bubbled over and I admit that I shrewishly snapped at the man. He had no right to speak to me, a stranger, in such a forward manner, and told him so in no uncertain terms. I felt my anger ignite and my face flush.

"Now, now," he protested. "See here; I mean you no disrespect, miss. It's only from experience I speak and kindness that I speed you on your way. Tha's all."

His hand, covered by an oily, disreputable-looking work glove, found my own and he gave it a pat. My temper, having already flared, regressed, but I allowed it to continue to lightly simmer on the back burner. I soon bid the man farewell and, full of directions to Janus House, I drove away from the filling station and headed north.

It was then that I noticed that the old man had, somehow without my knowledge, entwined a sprig of holly in my hood ornament.

The short approach to Janus House was a marvel. The town of Mount Airy opened into lengthy cornfields, which I presumed to be part of the grounds owned by the sergeant. Seeing them made me realize that I did not know of what regiment or even of what campaigns the man I sought had served in – or even if he was a real military man at all. Sadly, there where those individuals who claimed service to their country and veteran status but whose backgrounds were, to put it mildly, a bit spotty. Having immense pride in my own father and brothers' honorable service in the war, I sincerely hoped that Sgt. Janus was cut from the same stout cloth.

My eye transfixed by a murder of crows worrying a small songbird overhead, I almost wrecked my motorcar in a ditch as I navigated a curve in the road. Regaining control of the vehicle and my senses, there ahead of me, finally, was Janus House.

Knowing something of architecture, I spied and identified at least three or four different styles in its structure; it was an impressive thing indeed. Turrets and gables seemed to sprout like weeds along the mansion's façade, presenting a picture of a mad architect whose greed attempted to gobble up every known facet of the trade and incorporate them into a single edifice. Still, there was order present, too, and I found myself slowing down to take it all in. After what I originally perceived as only a moment's pause, I recognized I had been sitting stopped in my motorcar for several minutes while I viewed the face of Janus House.

Something inside of me leaped at the sight, yet, also, shrank back in what I can only describe as apprehension. Why? I asked myself. It was not a dreary place, not by any stretch of the imagination, but there was something foreboding about it, hiding between its shingles and crouching in the shadow of it eaves. I soldiered on.

I saw nowhere formal to park my vehicle, so I simply pulled up to the long stretch of stairs ascending to an impressive porch and shut off the motor. No one came out to greet me so I shouldered my bag and, sucking up a bit of courage from a stray thought of my father, I climbed the stairs to the porch and rang the bell.

While I waited, I glanced around my immediate vicinity. With windows blackened by heavy drapery, the porch was devoid of furniture save for what appeared to be a bootjack near the door; I certainly hoped I was not expected to remove my shoes before entering

4

the house! Certainly this was the custom in the Far East, from what I understood, but not here in the more civilized West. I told myself that the device was simply for equestrian friends of the sergeant and not for those who reached out to him with the problems inherent to his profession.

While I mused on these things, I had not noticed that the bell had been answered and the front door opened to reveal a most striking individual. I looked up at that moment to meet the most beautiful set of eyes I had yet ever encountered.

"Hello," said the woman in the doorway. Her voice was sibilant and rich, yet quiet. "You are expected. Please enter." She held the door and stepped to one side to allow me ingress. As I passed her my mind took stock of these things: she was shorter than myself by at least an inch and was clad in a long, midnight blue frock that was loose in the sleeves but perhaps a bit too form-fitting elsewhere for propriety's sake. Her hair was luster defined and straight, held in place by a clip at her left temple of some strange design I could not quite discern. Her scent was of lavender, yet also of a smoky tang I could not identify; as a woman myself, this caused me no small consternation. Her eyes…her eyes were cut glass, all blues and precious metals.

So enraptured by this women was I that I did not notice that she had shut the front door and had moved to clasp the knob of the door on the opposite side of the foyer. My eyes tracked her smooth movement, yes, but my brain did not register such movement. When I finally came to my senses, I watched as she cocked her head at me, as if listening for something, then glanced at the front door. She stood silently then, as if frozen. I turned to the door behind me, unsure of what was transpiring – if anything at all.

Presently, she afforded me a faint smile and, arching one raven eyebrow, opened the foyer door and went through it. I noticed that she did not invite or allow me to enter first.

I followed the woman into a hallway with a high cathedral ceiling and flowers everywhere. With all the blooms present, one might think the fragrance would have been overwhelming, yet they gave the hall a pleasant atmosphere with only a mild scent. I saw a staircase ascend to a landing ahead of me with open doorways to the right and the left. The only furniture was an umbrella stand just inside the foyer door and the only ornamentation was a merry-yet-not-ostentatious chandelier and a single painting. The work I guessed to be of the previous century and somewhat dark in its color palette. It held a certain appeal.

A thought nagged at me just then. I turned to the woman and inquired how it was that I was expected when I was certain that I had not confirmed to those who told me of the Sergeant that I would be calling on him. The woman smiled again and narrowed those beautiful eyes of sapphire and gold.

"Well, I was informed of your arrival and asked to greet you," she said, almost a whisper. "The sergeant will see you presently; that is, if you still wish him to receive you."

Before I could ask who it was that gave her the information, she turned on her heel with a faint rustle of skirts and disappeared through the doorway to the left. Alone, and the full weight of my reason for the visit now sitting squarely on my chest, I sighed and looked around the hallway, unsure of what exactly I should do. To leave after having invested the time and energy to arrive seemed a childish option, so I waited and listened.

The house was filled with sounds, if one was inclined to quiet their own thoughts and pick them out. Voices drifted in from the right, though interestingly not from the doorway. A conversation between two men, I guessed, or perhaps a man and a deep-voiced woman – regardless, it was congenial and amiable. Overhead I heard the sound of what I assumed to be machinery of some sort; a motorized fan or possibly even a vacuum of a kind? From the direction of the stairs I was quite sure I heard singing, though I was unable to pick out a recognizable tune from it. The doorway to the left, which had swallowed up my female host, issued only a faint gurgling sound, as that of water flowing through winding pipes. Put together, all these sounds spoke to more a living, breathing entity than a house of brick and wood.

The dark woman returned and, lightly taking my elbow, guided me through the doorway to the left. We traversed a long corridor with many doors, all of them shut, until we exited into a grand ballroom. It was a glorious room, filled with music though absent of any orchestra or even so much as a quartet. Above, a multitude of what appeared to be opera boxes dotted the walls and I wondered at such an architectural oddity. Again, the women took me by the arm and led me out of the room and into another long corridor, this one sans doors. From there we passed through a series of comfortable-looking dayrooms and into another corridor, this one stretching some distance. Surely the house couldn't be as large as all this?

Feeling slightly dizzy and with one particular painting we had passed of a small picnic on a rocky beach stuck in my head, I was guided into the most engaging little study or library I had ever seen.

I am a book person, if there ever was one, and God bless us every one. This storehouse of volumes reached out to me – that is the only way I can describe it – and took hold of my eyes and my nose and my fingertips and bade me come look. I turned to my guide and she smiled and nodded and turned to leave, only hesitating momentarily at the door as if transfixing my image in her mind and then exiting. As the door clicked softly closed behind her I set my bag down on an inviting, deeply-upholstered chair of red velvet and walked over to the nearest shelf of books, my heels clicking loudly on the highly-polished wood floor.

Before me stretched the most eclectic concentration of books ever known to civilization. Of this I am sure. I spied volumes on themes esoteric, esthetic, arcane and archaic; all that the common man would shrink from, I mused, but perhaps rightfully so. The bevy of titles and bindings made my head swim as I tried to read one after another – though many of them proved to be in languages wholly alien to me. Sgt. Janus' library thrilled me, yet also frightened me; here were subjects the world had largely forgotten.

The books bore titles such as *Grand Thoughts of the Mages*, *Prospectus Diabolus*, *Bushkill's Encyclopedia of Revenants*, *The Silent Spell* and a queer little publication with the perfectly chilling appellation of *Do Not Open This Book*.

Reaching out for a particularly interesting spine, a sharp pain struck in my head stalled my hand and I stopped to rub my temple. Hoping I was not succumbing to an illness, I continued to massage my forehead and contented myself with gazing across the many titles before me.

Then, he was suddenly beside me.

"I am Roman Janus. It is a pleasure to meet you."

Startled, for I had not in the slightest heard him enter the room, I took a quick step back and my heel skidded across the slick floor and I tumbled. Sgt. Janus' hand leapt out and caught mine and, gently righting me, he led me over to a chair of blue suede across from the one of red velvet. A bit dizzy, I fought to regain my composure and brushed away the pain in my head and my growing embarrassment. The sergeant waved a hand and tut-tutted.

"Never mind that," he said. "You're in a strange place and most likely, no, *most assuredly* are a bit bewildered by your surroundings. Would you care for a sherry?"

"I would rather a brandy, if you don't mind," I replied perhaps too quickly but, if I did so, he did not seem to notice and, while he fetched the snifter, I rearranged my skirts, suddenly feeling very exposed. He returned with the brandy and moved to take the chair across from me, but stopped when he saw my bag there. He smiled.

"May I?" he inquired, as if he felt required to ask in his own home.

I nodded, relishing the burn of the brandy on my tongue, and he gingerly moved my bag to a nearby ottoman and then sat. He seemed to sink back into the red velvet and I would swear in a court of law and on the Holy Bible that the chair somehow welcomed him and that he and it became one.

This was Sgt. Janus; a well-formed man of dusky blonde hair, trimmed short and neat but not too much so, and clean-shaven with a slightly-pointed chin but still very much a manly one. His eyes were icy verdigris but warm, also, and piercing – in a kind way. He was dressed smartly in a long coat of an almost military cut and dark pants with gold piping. His tall boots were most definitely of military origin and I thought suddenly of the bootjack on his front porch. His hands he held clasped in front of him in his lap, casually yet formally, too, as if weighing great problems while waiting for the weather to change. His fingers, I noticed, were long and supple and devoid of any decoration save a tiny band of what I thought might be copper on the smallest finger of his right hand.

Seeing the ring made me look back to his face for some reason and I noticed a very similar band of copper in his right ear. This was Sgt. Janus, enigmatic and electric yet cool and composed, too.

Now with this man as a focal point, I took notice of his immediate surroundings and saw there fashions and furnishings that echoed what I perceived to be his personality and tastes. I saw many objects from what I guessed to be foreign lands and of ancient vintage. Cubes and lobes and carvings and gimcracks and gewgaws of frenzied variety, all of them vying for my attention, competing with the mysterious tomes that dominated the study. I saw also souvenirs of war: cannonballs and muskets, swords and bayonets, carbines and claymores.

And in the middle of all this sat Sgt. Janus. He saw me take notice of him again, finally, and smiled. It reminded me of the women who greeted me. He cleared his throat and spoke.

"I apologize for not being able to greet you when you first arrived, but I sit before you now and would be glad to hear of your problem."

I asked him what it was exactly that he did. His smile faded and a more serious countenance took its place.

"I break spirits," he said.

His eyes twinkled then. "Oh, you needn't look at me like that. I don't mean, of course, the indomitable will of man – I don't believe that can ever be truly broken – but rather the wily essence of mankind that lingers on after death and, eschewing its final reward, chooses to stay and vex the living.

"You see, the ancients –" He looked around the room at this moment. "– were ever so much more closely tied to the spirit world, and *understood it*. Lived with it. Why, even embraced it, I suppose. Modern man…well, let's just say we're more frightened of the dark

9

today to a degree that far surpasses the superstitions of our ancestors."

His voice was clear and controlled, but underneath it I discerned a slight rasp, as if he has long ago suffered an injury to his throat. He spoke with conviction and a hint of both amusement and ruefulness, as if chagrinned at his forebears. I cleared my own throat, now unexpectedly eager to tell him of my situation….despite the growing weight upon me.

"My name is Miss Catherine Pym," I began, watching his eyes watch me. "Perhaps you know of my family, the Ulster Pyms? My father is Colonel Brewster Pym, retired, and one of the greatest men I have ever known. Though I was schooled abroad, and the colonel often remarking too much so, it did little to squelch my natural tendencies. You see, they say I take after my father in some matters of temperament."

Sgt. Janus nodded at that, a slight smile playing around the corners of his mouth.

"I am engaged to be married this October 1st to a lovely man – Jonathan Drew. I recently took a sabbatical from my teaching duties at the university and we have spent the last three months searching for a house to live in once we are married. I must admit not having much luck at it. Then, when we had all but acknowledged our defeat at the hands of fate, a house just outside the city came on the market and we fell wildly in love with it. Both of us, perhaps Jonathan even more so.

"It was not a big house but it was rich with character and it seemed to reflect our personalities. Jonathan insisted on having it decorated by a renowned artist of our acquaintance and made me promise to stay away while he and our friend labored over the furnishings. I suppose he wanted to surprise me, and I suppose I loved him even more for that, but, well, a woman's curiosity is an evil, evil thing and I couldn't help but take a small peek one day while he was away on business. That was when everything truly began, I suppose. My troubles, that is."

I believe my voice broke when I had reached that point in my story, but Sgt. Janus' face never showed any surprise or disdain at it, only a more pointed concentration. I felt sure that he had begun to examine me wholly at that moment, body and soul, though his eyes never wavered from my face. My feeling of exposure became even more acute and I resisted the overwhelming urge to pull my jacket more tightly around me and my skirts farther to the floor. That in itself bothered me, for though a lady I have never been overly demure.

"I drove up to the house one late afternoon, about three weeks ago, and feeling a bit mischievous entered and set about in exploration. Oh, Jonathan and our artist friend had done wonders with its rooms – a testament to his determination, for the house was already from the beginning a real wonder. He had invested its spaces with such charm and style that I thanked goodness he was not there at that moment for I may have crushed the life out of him with my appreciation.

"I walked through the house, marveling at the décor and the furnishings and yes, feeling a bit guilty, just a tad, at being such a devil and breaking my promise to Jonathan. Still, I was satisfied that I was championing all women's curiosity in doing so and I reveled in the thought of the life we would have together in the house."

Here I stopped in my exposition and collected my thoughts. Sgt. Janus said nothing, and waited patiently for me to continue. I began to feel more comfortable in his presence, despite his scrutiny. He sat forward in his chair and steepled his hands below his chin.

"As I walked through the house I began to feel…well, I…I'm not sure. As if I was being watched? No, no that's too strong. As if I weren't alone? That, too, is not entirely accurate, but suffice to say I began to feel a bit *odd* and I chalked it up to guilt over disobeying my fiancé. But, I must say, that didn't stop me from looking into every nook and cranny of the house while I was there.

"I'm ashamed to say I don't know much of the history of the place, but I do know that it was a relatively young structure, having only been built roughly twenty years or so before. We were told it had only one previous owner who had divorced his wife and mysteriously sailed overseas to start anew, presumably. Jonathan and I weren't much interested in the house's history, only in our own future therein.

"After an hour or two in the house it began to grow dark outside and, discovering that the utilities were not yet turned on, I planned to leave before the shadows grew long and I wouldn't be able to see my hand before my face. But, I stayed. In fact, it began to rain that evening and I decided to stay the night. I will regret that decision for the rest of my life."

I paused again there and afraid to meet Sgt. Janus' gaze I stared down at the hem of my skirt and silently willed the man not to speak. At that moment I was entirely afraid, perhaps even terrified at what he would say – or what I would say in return.

"Miss Pym," he said, softly. "Forgive me for asking, but you said 'was,' did you not?"

I looked up at him to find a most fascinating and somewhat strange look on his handsome face. "I'm sorry – what?"

He reached out and took my hand. His eyes flickered momentarily to my throat and them back up to my face. "You said the house *was* not big, *was* relatively young. Why do you speak of it in the past tense?"

Blinking back tears and cursing myself, I looked him square in the eye. "Because, Sgt. Janus, that next morning I burnt it to the ground."

What he said next took me eminently by surprise. "Are you familiar with Portobello Road, Miss Pym?

A bit taken back by this inquiry, I chuckled – most likely a very rude thing to do – and admitted that while the name was familiar to me, its particulars were not.

"It's a street in London, a most wonderful street, though calling it simply a 'street' does not do it one modicum of justice. It is a place of dreams, Miss Pym, an Aladdin's Cave of treasures. On Portobello Road you may find anything and everything you are searching for. And a few things you may never even imagined. I dare say half… no…a goodly portion of the volumes in this room were bought on that very street. I have unearthed rarities there of a kind that no ordinary booksellers would stock, let alone possess knowledge of. When I am not at my work, I am making my way to Portobello Road – either in reality or in my dreams.

"Well, anyway, one day a cobbler who made the most amazing footwear at a little cart on the street found a gem tucked down deep in a shoe that he had crafted only the day before. Unsure of what do about his amazing find – was it truly his to keep? – he hid it away in his sack and planned to later take it to a jeweler friend of his on the street for appraisal. The cobbler never did learn the value of the gem, save for recognizing its supposed value to the fiend who cut his throat a second or so before he died.

"That cutthroat then fell prey to another cutthroat – there is truly no honor whatsoever among thieves, Miss Pym – and from there to another and eventually it rolled and tumbled into the hands of a young girl, an orphan who lived on Portobello Road and begged there every day. She fell in love with the gem and did a very, very strange thing with it."

As he talked I had an odd sensation fell upon me, as if I were being engulfed by something, or enveloped. Warm and almost fetid, it spread about my person from a central point in front of me. Sgt. Janus' words held my attention but I could not wholly ignore the creeping *something* that spread out and over me.

"The little girl," he continued, "held up the gem for all to see, presuming her safety would be insured by sharing her find with all. Clever little thing, she endeared herself to the vendors and customers of Portobello Road who one and all flocked to see her treasure.

"People began to notice that the gem was transfixed by an image of sorts, a variation in its color that resembled, or so they said, a seaborne creature. A whale, or perhaps even a porpoise..."

As he said this, I felt another stabbing pain in my head and I found myself tightly gripping the front of my jacket. Looking up at the man, he appeared to change before my eyes, slowly, into a wholly different thing.

"The gem became a sensation," said Janus. "They called it the 'Portobello Cetacean' and it and the girl were pampered and protected, and no one dared to separate them. Though its true origins have never been uncovered, some have said the gem came from as far away as Austria-Hungary and that ancient druids had toiled for years to etch the shape in its core. Imagine: persons of a land-locked country having knowledge of a mighty monster of the deep such as a whale.

"Then, quite horrendously, the little girl was found murdered one day, her throat slit from ear to ear and the Cetacean gone. Taken. Vanished. The street flew into an uproar and the wailing was said to be able to be heard in far-off Scotland. So loved was the girl and so fiendish the crime that men were heard to curse the murderer, whoever he was, and damn him for all eternity. This in itself is not enough for true damnation, of course, but a priest, who was said to visit the girl every day, laid down his vows and, standing over the pooling blood of the girl, called upon the Almighty to curse the gem and the murderer and to damn them both.

"They say that God slew the priest there and then, and that He also laid an unmovable shadow across the Portobello Cetacean and those whose hands it would fall into, forever more."

My hands shook as he finished his tale and perspiration beaded on my forehead and down my cheeks. He looked at me, leaden eyes boring into mine and then to the pendant I wore on a chain around my neck and close to my heart. I swear he had horns then. I swear it.

"Miss Pym, where did you get that gem?" he asked.

"From…Jonathan," I answered. "Jonathan gave it to me upon our engagement."

"Ah," he said simply, "I see." Then, he reached out and grabbed my shoulders and I tried to shrug myself loose from him. Or *something* did. Perhaps it wasn't me at all. I truly do not know.

"That night, alone in the house," I slurred. "I heard voices. I saw…things. I don't want to remember them. It was the longest night of my life and in the morning I found petrol and rags and I burned it to the ground – and in doing so I lost my Jonathan! He will not speak to me! He will not have anything to do with me! I do not know what I shall do with myself!"

Sgt. Janus' crystal eyes darted back and forth from my own to the Cetacean clutched now in my hands, as if searching for a sign that it was one and the same from his story. His calm manner was eroding; I could see that. Finally, he narrowed his eyes and then jumped up suddenly from his chair.

"Come!" he shouted, with a voice that seemed to roll and echo in the room. "Come, Catherine – come with me this instant!" And he grabbed my hands and rushed me to the door and through it and down the long corridor.

Our flight seemed to never end, through corridors and doorways, past rooms and halls, and over many a staircase. I am sure we went both *up* and *down* many times and quite possibly passed the same spots in the great manor more than once. If you asked me to draw a plan of Janus House, I would admit defeat. I no longer knew where I was, or what hour it was. I no longer was sure of anything, including, most supremely, who I had become. I knew only a dull heat in my chest and a growing hatred for Sgt. Janus.

Feverish, confused and dazed, he pulled me up suddenly in front of a door of paneled oak which he proceeded to fling open and rush me through. Inside was a darkened room that seemed to have no windows and no other doors, but did possess dark walls that appeared to be fashioned like cushions. In the middle of the room I caught a glimpse of a kind of bench or table with the same sort of cushioning on it. Sgt. Janus all but threw me into the room and slammed shut the door behind us, bolting it and making sure it was secure. Turning to me, I saw a most curious look on his face, one that terrified me to the core. He stalked towards me and I backed up, feeling the table against the back of my legs. There was nowhere to go.

He reached for me, with what I perceived to be claws and I lost consciousness as I fell backwards onto the table.

A grinning face loomed out of the darkness, insanity etched into its every pore. I raised my hands to fend it off but could not, as my arms were bags of lead filings and my head a sack of potatoes. Then, I am quite sure that in a rush of anxiety mixed with anger I struck something…or someone. Loud voices assailed my ears – someone was shouting at me in a booming tone. I remember thinking of the gem, that the gem must be protected at all cost, that it was somehow my salvation.

Again, I lashed out and felt my fists connect with something. Even now, the realization sickens me.

God help me! I thought, but I was sure then that He had forsaken me in His infinite wisdom. So be it. I was set on fire and my senses ripped from me once again.

Some time later, I awoke.

I know not how long I was in the arms of Morpheus. That portion of my stay at Janus House is perhaps lost to me forever. Suffice to say I awoke in a strange room, but not the one in which I last saw Sgt. Janus. This was a cheery room, with a delicate flower pattern in the wallpaper and homey pieces of furniture here and there. I found myself stretched out on a settee, apparently having been dozing there for quite some time.

I sensed something amiss and, sitting up, discovered my jacket gone, the first two buttons of my blouse loosened and one shoe missing. Further, my stocking on the exposed foot was torn and my large toe stuck through the rent. Panic spread through me and I rifled through my memories for answers.

The raven-tressed woman who first ushered me into the great house was suddenly by my side, kneeling down to take hold of my hands and gently urging me to lie back again. She smiled, looking at me with pity and care.

"I assure you there was no impropriety, Miss Pym," she said. "Your host regrets the loss of your jacket but it was unavoidable, given the circumstances."

Continuing to sense my thoughts, or perhaps to outright read my mind, she reached down and retrieved my shoe from next to the settee. Holding it up to show me that my footwear fared much better than my jacket, she then turned her head to draw my attention to the small table that sat to one side. There upon it lay the remains of my pendant – and the Portobello Cetacean.

The gem had been shattered somehow, and the gold of the surrounding pendant and chain blackened. Someone had taken the pains to scoop up what appeared to be very small pieces of the gem

16

and lay them out on the table. As proof, perhaps? As a warning? A moral? I do not know.

The dark woman ran her hand across my brow and I divined her intention to speak. Lying back against the comfortable pillows of the settee I silently bade her to do so.

"Sgt. Janus also regrets the destruction of your pendant but that too was wholly unavoidable. You see, it held a very vexing spirit.

"When you began to tell him of your troubles he sensed immediately that you had not arrived at his home alone. No, he saw as you talked that you had a spirit hiding inside you. Yes, *you*, Miss Pym. Not the gem, but your own self. His story of the Portobello Cetacean was a ruse to keep the spirit focused on the bauble and not on trying to hide itself from him. He is sorry he could not allow you to know of his ruse, but he saw that this spirit was so connected with your own life energy that anything you knew, *it* would know, too.

"Confirming the presence of the spirit and determining that it was one that meant you no good, he knew he must break it. So, he regaled you with the tale of the Cetacean to lure the entity into a trap – one that played out most satisfactorily. Once he felt the spirit was 'on the ropes,' so to speak, he whisked you off to the Room of Confrontation. Yes, he had to further confuse the spirit by taking a very non-direct path to his destination and unfortunately, my dear Miss Pym, he in turn had to ensnare you in that self-same confusion. I hope you may find it in your heart to forgive him all that he has put you through – but the culmination was the destruction of much evil.

"You undoubtedly felt the rising anger and perhaps even hatred of the spirit inside you, yes? Sgt. Janus felt this was so, further assuming you were also entering into the hallucinatory phase of the possession and knew there was no time to waste in exorcising you of your unwanted occupant. In the Room of Confrontation, he continued with the ruse of the Cetacean and urged the spirit to take possession of the gem, suggesting it was a greater source of evil and a much better vehicle for deviltry than your body.

"The gambit worked, and once inside your gem and away from you, he destroyed the bauble and with it the entity. That which you see on the table there is all that is left of your troubles. Sgt. Janus offers his personal assurance of that fact."

Taking in all that the woman had told me, I came close to tears then. Not from sadness or from fear, but from relief, as if a great, great weight had been lifted from me and I was free to live the rest of my life in peace. I realized that since the fire I had felt an increasing strain upon my person, but without knowing its source. But, many question still remained.

"Who was this spirit?" I asked. "Why did it seek to inhabit me?"

The woman looked thoughtful. "We do not know its identity, but for a certainty it resided in the house that your fiancé bought for you and with which he intended to make a nest for your shared love. Your unguarded presence that night in the house gave it the opportunity to perhaps spread its evil in a much greater range. Sgt. Janus suspects that in life it was a person of great mischief and a doer of malevolent deeds. These traits often follow a personality into the grave – and beyond. You were simply there, Miss Pym, and unknowing of the supernatural, you were the perfect vehicle for it."

I pressed on. "My jacket? My stocking?"

"The spirit attacked the sergeant," she replied. "Making good use of your arms and hands, I'm afraid. Your jacket was shredded by its exertions – and when it was finally quelled your rescuer drew it out as it had first entered you: through your feet, most precisely the great toe on your right foot. Legend tells us that evil is enamored of the feet, as the serpent lost his own after the temptation of the First Woman.

"How do you feel now?" she then inquired.

I told her that, despite all that I had been through in the preceding hours, I felt fine and that I should recover quite nicely, thank you ever so much. I sat up and swung my feet to the floor and recovered my missing shoe. Rebuttoning my blouse I reached for my jacket and then, remembering, I smoothed out my skirts and shook out my hair.

"Sgt. Janus sends along his best wishes to you and is sorry he cannot join you at this time," she noted. "If you are ready, I will show you to your motorcar."

Looking down upon my shattered pendant, I mused over the pieces of the gem. "One more question," said I. "The Portobello Cetacean – was it a true story? About the little girl and the priest? And the curse?"

The woman with the black, lustrous hair smiled at me, almost as if a parent to a child. "Some things are better left unsaid, Miss Pym."

I write this from my honeymoon abroad, a day after my wedding. Jonathan has returned to me and my life is now complete. Once I left Janus House I sought him out and, when he saw me approach, no words were exchanged between us but it was as if he sensed that I was once again myself. He ran to me and kissed me and swore his undying love. The wedding plans proceeded anew.

When the letter from Janus House arrived weeks later asking me to provide this document, I was happy do so; as I stated previously, it would provide me with an accounting of my experiences. Supposedly, Sgt. Janus does not record his cases himself but relies on his clients for documentation – an odd method of conducting his career but, then again, there is much that is odd about him and his profession. I gather that he may appreciate a different point-of-view of his work than his own. Also, I had expected a bill for his services to be included in the letter, but no such bill arrived then nor since.

There was also a small note, written in a crisp, formal style that I took to be that of the sergeant. It said:

"My dear Miss Pym, you are a very brave and steadfast woman and it has been a pleasure to have made your acquaintance. Without your stamina, your beautiful inner strength, the day might have been lost. I hope you will take some comfort in that. Also, you fight like the clanswomen of the Scottish Highlands. God go with you."

I wish I could have thanked Sgt. Janus personally for all that he has done for me and, most especially, the danger in which he had placed himself on my behalf. I do not know why he does what he does, combating the supernatural – or is it simply the unknown? – for those who cannot themselves take up arms against it.

When the dark woman, whose name I never did learn, was guiding me back to the entrance hall we passed the door of Sgt. Janus' study and, looking through the slightly-cracked door, I believe I saw the man himself, or a pale, wispy image of him, sitting in his red velvet chair with head in hands and exuding an air of exhaustion and reflection. I think I know now the heavy toll such combat takes upon such soldiers. God bless him.

Here, at the end of the tale, I am still unsure of the exact width and breadth of all that transpired, but I sense, despite the dream I described at the beginning, that I am free of evil. Perhaps despite any lingering dark dreams, a life suffused with ghosts is not such a bad life after all, and so I close this record of my experiences as a happy woman.

Thank you.

'SPIRIT-BREAKER' NABS CROOKS

At approximately 3:40 on the morning of May 29, Mount Airy police officers took one Kenneth Shabbinski, of No. 8 Genesee Avenue, into custody. He was subsequently charged with breaking-and-entry as well as assault at the Jehovah Precinct Station. Mr. Shabbinski was seen to have had bruising on his face and a broken finger on his left hand.

Deputy Police Commissioner Dimple told our reporter that officers were called to the Playdium Theater at 1958 Front Street in the early morning hours by a complaint from the owner of a neighboring establishment, the Bells & Whistles. The complaint concerned "strange noises, like moans and shrieks" issuing from the Playdium. The complainant, who had stayed open late for the holiday, said that he knew the theater had closed for the night and that no such noises should be heard on its premises while not open for business.

Upon entering the premises, the officers encountered one Sgt. Roman Janus, of No. 4 Raynham Road, who claimed he was "investigating a spirit infestation" at the Playdium. The officers recognized the sergeant as Mount Airy's well-known "spirit-breaker," a reputed hunter of ghosts, and a frequent police consultant. Determining that Janus was not the source of the noises, they were then confronted with Mr. Shabbinski and a lady friend, Miss Idalene Montrose, of no fixed address. The gentlemen told the officers that he and Miss Montrose had been imbibing heavily not an hour or so before and that they had "slipped into the theater for a bit of fun." He further explained that this was the source of the odd sounds heard by the owner of the Bells & Whistles. Sgt. Janus then reportedly informed the officers that Mr. Shabbinski was, in fact, lying and that he was on the premises to rob the Playdium's box office of its receipts. These accusations were supported, said Janus, by "messages from the spirit world," given to the sergeant on the spot.

Mr. Shabbinski took umbrage to the accusations and assaulted the sergeant. Before the officers could act, Janus had defended himself and produced bruising on his assailant's face and broken his finger. Mr. Shabbinski was then taken into custody and later charged. Miss Montrose was also apprehended and charged with aiding and abetting. Bail has not yet been set for either of the accused.

After the incident, Sgt. Janus told the police that "the Playdium is a vortex of immeasurable super-natural proportions" and that it "must be sealed off for fear of further spirit infiltration." No further investigation by the police has occurred.

From *The Mount Airy Eagle*
Early Edition - Tuesday, May 29

Chapter II
A BAD BUSINESS

I should like to state here at the beginning of this account that I write it somewhat under duress. I feel it is an imposition to the client of a business – no matter what sort of business – that he should have to provide his own record of his transaction. It is exceedingly fortunate for Mr. Janus that I am currently convalescing after having fractured my leg and possess a certain amount of charitable time to give to this document.

I also question the very nature of the man's business and feel at this time that there are certain elements of our transaction which are questionable. In all the years as a businessman myself, I have never experienced such rudeness, such impenetrable gall, on the part of a proprietor of a firm.

To the point, my name is Randolph Rushkin, Jr., and I own and operate Rushkin Worldwide, Ltd., a shipping concern of some note. It is a company with an exceptional reputation and I invite anyone to view our credentials and tell me it isn't so. We cater to all sorts of clientele, but most especially so to those with specific requirements in their shipping needs. "No Package Too Big, No Package Too Small" is Rushkin's motto.

Our offices are located at the corner of Pine and Grimm in the city, in a grand old building that suits our own needs perfectly. Many other such businesses are quartered in insufficient offices and that shows in their operations. Rushkin Worldwide has proudly operated out of our present site for more than eighty-five years.

Now, to the heart of the matter: As October wound to a close, my firm worked at closing out our books for the month and all was as it usually was; my staff is efficient, no stragglers, and all seemed normal. Then, the disturbances began.

I say "disturbances" because I do not know how else to describe the events. Suffice to say that they were of growing consternation to me as they threatened to disrupt the exacting flow of commerce through my company. Some small things around the offices began to disappear, both office material and personal effects belonging to my employees. I suspected that a local youth, one of the urchins that panhandles on the street outside our firm, had gained access to the offices somehow and helped himself to the "booty."

Then, and quite frustratingly, a few pieces of furniture were found to be broken. A chair, an electric fan, a typewriter – even the glass in my own private office's door was discovered to be cracked right down the middle one morning. This was intolerable, of course, and I brought the matter up with the police and urged them to dispense more patrolmen at night to watch the building. They seemed to humor me, a completely unsatisfactory response to a businessman of my standing and reputation.

The crowning injustice arrived one particular morning when my office manager told me, quite embarrassingly so, that the firm's safe had been tampered with.

Rushkin Worldwide is very proud of our safe; an immense piece of work, it is large enough to walk into and is of a caliber that would make any bank green with envy. The night before the incident in question, I set the tumblers and the wheel just so, and the next morning my manager found the entire works awry. To say I was not happy with this turn of events would be an understatement.

So angered was I that I ordered my manager to call the police himself, as I was in no condition to speak with them again – and quite assuredly be humored again. In an unspeakable state I fled from the offices to air my temper and give me time to think. My flight took me to The Dawntreader, a small tavern of my acquaintance not far from Rushkin Worldwide.

There, and with a good whiskey in front of me and a cigar for cognitive clarity, I chided myself for my reaction. It is not like me to leave the offices during work hours and especially not to drink during the daytime. The disturbances, I must admit, had broken my orderly patterns and the thought troubled me. So too did the very next thoughts that occurred to me.

For some odd reason I remembered something one of my employees, a Jonathan Drew, told me. It seems he and his new bride had some sort of "disturbance" themselves earlier in the year, and the girl had appealed to a local doctor or some such for aid. Fixed things right up, or so young Mr. Drew claimed, but he remained vague on what exactly this man did for them. Nothing short of "miraculous," Drew said, and if he wasn't one of the finest young businessmen I've had the pleasure to mentor I wouldn't have given it much credence. There are far too many shysters and flim-flam operators in this world and far too little sense among the general populace to see through them.

Regardless, as I sat in The Dawntreader I remembered Drew's words and wondered about them anew. The very thought of airing my concerns about the office's difficulties to someone other than the police was not a comfortable one, and besides, what could this doctor or whatever he was, actually do? To make matters even more insoluble, Drew and his bride were on their honeymoon at the time and unreachable; they had the man's whereabouts and I did not.

Then, incredibly, I looked up and there he was.

Yes, the coincidence was a staggering one and one I surely hate to acknowledge, but I cannot deny what I experienced then and there in that tavern. I was presented with the very man whose existence I had just pondered.

Even more incredibly, I had no concrete evidence at to his identity. Looking up from my reverie, I saw a man enter the tavern, one whose very presence muted the noise of the place by much more than a hair. He was dressed in a kind of military-style jacket and lustrous riding boots that immediately raised my hackles – I have known those among us who wear the trappings of service to one's country but have never served themselves. It is an abomination to the true soldiers, the veterans of war, and I count myself among them. I was sure that this man did not deserve to sport such attire, but, strangely, I felt certain this was the person that my employee had mentioned.

I was dissecting his appearance – the rough-and-tumble kind some women are enamored with, I am told – when the man paused, looked over at me and, meeting my eye, stepped over to my solitary booth.

He begged my forgiveness for interrupting my solitude – as well he should – and introduced himself as Sgt. Roman Janus. I bristled at the mention of rank, but being a gentleman and a businessman I accepted his hand. It was smooth, as I suspected it would be, and I was sure he hadn't done a day's work in his life. His age I'd be hard-pressed to determine but suffice to say he seemed in his fourth decade and in good health. He smiled and asked if he could join me.

For the record, I want to state that I am unaccustomed to having strangers join me for a meal or even for simply a drink. I have few friends and no "loved ones," and go through life with no great thought to it. Something of this "Sgt." Janus intrigued me and I could not deny the overwhelming coincidence of our meeting. I mutely motioned for him to sit.

The man's rudeness manifested almost immediately as he looked at me rather pointedly and asked what my troubles might be.

"Mister Janus," I began. "I don't know you, sir, but being a prominent businessman with a prestigious firm hereabouts, perhaps you may know of *me*. I assure you that Rushkin Worldwide is a successful business and operates free from 'troubles,' thank you very much."

If he took umbrage of my dispensing of his "rank" he gave no notice of it, but only smiled that damnable smile of his. He asked my forgiveness again and said that he was more concerned for my *own* troubles. There was something in the way he asked; no, something in his voice? I can't be sure but quite against my will I began to tell him of the disturbances.

To the man's credit, he listened well and didn't interrupt. I stopped short of detailing any specific business practices of my firm, but laid out the problem, as it where. Janus then sat back when I had finished and closed his eyes. I thought for a moment that he had fallen asleep! Momentarily, he opened them and, sitting up, leaned in closer to me, almost conspiratorially, and said the most impertinent thing. He said they "wanted attention."

"To whom do you refer, sir?" I enquired. "Really, this is all very intolerable. You invade a man's solitary thoughts, ask impossible questions and make impenetrable statements. What's your game? Who are 'they'?"

Janus lost a bit of his patent smile and narrowed his eyes. For a quick moment I thought he might be taken aback at my words, but he pressed forward and topped his previous offerings by asking me if there had been deaths recently in my personal life or within my firm!

For me, at that moment, the interview was finished. I had a business to run and customers to serve and had no time for parlor games and mumbo-jumbo. This faux-soldier with his annoying smile and unkempt hair had sorely tested my patience. I stood up and bid him a good day.

The man frowned and, standing up himself, rudely caught my arm. Into my hand he pressed a card and, looking me in the eye once again, asked that I pay a call on him at his home as soon as my schedule permitted.

Loosening his grip on my arm, I turned on my heel and, in exiting, put the entire business behind me.

The following Saturday, I found myself driving out to Mount Airy. I realize that it may seem to be the complete opposite to how I have portrayed myself to this point, but, well, I cannot explain it. Or, explain it in any convincing fashion, even to myself.

The small town of Mount Airy was not familiar to me, save that it rested some two hours distance from the city and held no real interest to a businessman such as myself. I suppose one should accept that a need for shipping could come from any quarter, but if I had my measure of the citizens of Mount Airy, there was little business to be found there.

Janus House rested a short stretch from the town and, after verifying my directions from the proprietor of a service station nearby – a thorough yet somewhat unwholesome old gentleman – I pulled up in front of my destination. Doubt filled me as I viewed the structure and I wondered if I was in the right place. The entire house was of a rambling, ill-designed sort and I guessed that its architect had devoted more time to opium than his plans. But then, remembering the unorthodox man I met in The Dawntreader, I felt certain then that my aim was true.

Fortunately, the sight of the ramshackle mansion was tempered by being greeted at the door by the most exquisite creature I've ever had the distinct pleasure to meet.

She was a smoky thing, at once nebulous and then quite charmingly solid. Done up in a long black dress that fetchingly matched her raven tresses she seemed almost a shadow until she raised her clear, white face to me and smiled. Her eyes seemed as if they had been mined from precious metals, rather than grown organically; they bewitched me. I should say no more here for fear that she may spy this document. Suffice to say, I wanted to know more about her.

Sadly, she had few words for me but ushered me inside and, after taking my coat, hat and cane, disappeared from view. Left alone, I attempted to discern what it was about Janus House that had immediately begun to unsettle me.

This Janus' tastes ran to what some might call "eclectic," but which I call somewhat slovenly. Unmatched furniture vied with artwork and other furnishings of questionable origin; I know quality merchandise from my long experience in shipping goods around the globe and this house's trappings did not impress me. Furthermore, the music that reached my ears from some other part of the house was discordant and altogether unpleasant. To make matters worse, someone was having a rather loud conversation nearby that only added to the chaos. I hoped to spend little time in the structure; let the man appear and let us get this thing over with, I thought.

That stunning female form in black joined me again – seemingly from nowhere! – and had me follow her. As we walked down a corridor I guessed we were near the kitchens as I smelled cooking meats and what I assumed to be a boiling fruit mash of a sort. The two scents did not compliment each other. Thankfully, they fell back and away as the woman and I walked further down the passageway. I began to feel quite lost then when we pulled up short in front of a smallish door and she told me that Janus waited inside.

I had come far, I felt, and for reasons that perplexed me, but that diminutive door almost broke me. Why, it surely grew smaller as I walked through it! Stooping farther than a man of my age and stature should, I made my way into the room beyond. There I found my host and a most strange and startling scene.

Janus was standing in front of what I would normally have referred to as a shooting range, save that there were no rifles or pistols in sight, only crossbows. Dressed almost identically as when I met him in the tavern, the man hefted a weighty-looking specimen of the weapons and was aiming it in my direction! Unsure of what I had walked into, I stopped and protested the attention.

That infuriating smile of his played across his lips and he lowered the crossbow. Apologizing that he was only setting the quarrel at the moment I entered, he set the piece on a nearby rack and offered me a chair. Quite sure that there was no chair when I first entered, I was amazed to see two of them along with a small table, off to one side. I assumed the shock of being targeted by the lethal-looking weapon made me overlook them.

"Mr. Rushkin," said my host after we had seated ourselves. "I thank you for joining me here today. I acknowledge your unwillingness to do so, but I feel as if I can truly help you with the problems at your firm."

Again, I called his entire manner impertinent but he offered me a drink and whatever could be said about the man, and I had much to say, he poured an exceptionally good brandy.

Janus then asked me to tell him more about Rushkin Worldwide, Ltd.

"I am a modest man, Mr. Janus," I said. "But I am very proud of my company. It was founded almost ninety years ago by my grandfather, Jasper Rushkin, but it didn't truly become a viable concern until my father, Randolph Rushkin, Sr., took over the business. Father had a keen mind for figures and practicalities that, sadly, eluded my grandfather, and he made Rushkin Worldwide one of the leading firms in national and international shipping. Our name is synonymous with thoroughness and timeliness. And affordability, I might add.

"Furthermore, I let nothing stand in the way of business – nothing. No man or force of nature, if you will. Reality is my concern, not superstition or the so-called 'super-natural'."

The man wasted no time with his interrogation. "Mr. Rushkin, I asked you the other day if there had been any deaths around you recently, and though you may continue to label me 'impertinent,' it's a query that must be answered if I'm to help you. Won't you humor me, sir, and answer it?"

Before making the sojourn to his home, I had made discreet inquiries though my military contacts and had learned that there was no "Sergeant Roman Janus" on any of the rolls of any of the branches of service, either active or retired. I supposed he could have been part of any one of the few special, circumspect branches, those not known to the public, but I highly doubted it. Whatever he was, I was sure that the man had no real claim to the rank he paraded about on his card.

But if he must have my answer, he must have it, I thought, and clearing my throat, I allowed him the information - though what he could do with it I did not know. "Not recently, no," I replied. "My father passed away almost twelve years ago. Before that, there had been a few deaths on the staff, yes, but he had kept several employees for many years, for they had been loyal and reliable and he was a stickler for that. As am I. You see, I grew up in those offices, quite literally, and learned the entire business at the side of my father and his staff. In some ways, they were the only real family I had."

I could feel my face flush at that admission and I silently cursed myself for it; what was it of this Janus that I offered up something that I had never told another living soul?

"I see," he said, simply and with no recognition of my embarrassment. "Spirits often remain connected, tethered if you will, to a place they knew in life. A place in which they spent a great deal of time or to which they had a strong attachment. I presume your disturbances to be caused by such spirits, as it fits the eternal pattern. They seek your attention."

What could I say to such a pronouncement? The card he had handed me at the tavern listed his profession as "Spirit-Breaker," and I assumed it was this sort of "spirit" he referred to. The bile rose in my throat and Janus must have sensed it.

"I thank you for your honesty, Mr. Rushkin," he soothed. "But I'm afraid I must beg your indulgence a bit more, for there are other important facts I must uncover today before I see through to a solution."

Then, he asked me the most impertinent, the most outrageous question of all.

"Can you tell me of your mother and the circumstances of her death?"

I'd had enough, and told him so. Standing, I declined to thank him for his hospitality, such as it was, and chalking it all up to a bad bit of business, left Janus House and its master to their own devices.

After two near-sleepless nights, I returned to the offices Monday morning. My secretary commented on my somewhat worse-for-wear appearance and, ignoring her, I ensconced myself in my private room. I had hoped that immersing myself in Rushkin Worldwide would serve to dispel thoughts of my weekend sojourn, but it did not.

I was barely behind my desk for 30 minutes when a framed certificate for merit from the city's business council fell off the wall and shattered on the floor. No, strike that: it *leaped* off the wall. I can describe it in no other way.

I was determined to ignore it. The only spirits at my firm where those that rose up when I handed out the yearly Christmas bonus to my workers. I would not let a complete stranger tell me that a settling building and a few mice in the walls were in fact hobgoblins. I was not a gullible child. My secretary then appeared at my office door and told me I had a caller. She handed me his card and, looking at it, saw that it was that of my old friend, "Sgt." Janus.

Not wishing to allow the man into my personal sanctum sanctorum, I rose and strode out into the larger room and to the front door. There stood Janus, a longcoat over his regular attire and no smile whatsoever to be found on his face. I saw his eyes taking in the room and everything in it.

"Mr. Rushkin," said he, not reaching out a hand in greeting. "I'm sorry our meeting on Saturday was cut short, but after much deliberation at my home, I came here to see if I may be of service in the afflicted area."

I chuckled ruefully to myself. Was the man a dullard? Could he not by now have realized my complete chagrin at his supposed profession, his empty "knowledge"? I pulled him off to one side and turned him away from the increasing number of my employees who had taken notice of the man.

"Mr. Janus," I whispered. "I have no need for you in any capacity. Do I make myself clear? We are open for business, as you can see, and I do not need any interruptions of this or any other sort – please leave, sir."

"I see," he nodded. "Unfortunately, you do not. I cannot say that you or your staff is in any particular danger, but the situation here will only grow worse if I do not attend to it. Just standing here, I can feel the etheric energies straining to be loose, not a desirable atmosphere for a successful and thriving business such as this."

I was sure he thought to skewer me where I live with that last comment, but I was in no mood to play at his game. With another idiotic word I would summon the police and have him removed.

"There is the door, sir," I pointed. "Leave."

Suddenly, a loud crash resounded from the far side of the room and I looked over to see that a filing cabinet had fallen over. One of my employees who had been standing next to it looked searchingly back at me, as if to protest his innocence and ask how such a thing could have happened. I swung my head back to Janus, but the man was gone.

Feeling then as if I had the full picture on the "Spirit-Breaker," I spent the rest of the day in my office, planning and scheming.

I knew, somehow *knew* for a certainty, that he'd be back and most likely by the end of the business day. I saw the look in his eye, that of knowing and of having the measure of the supposed "problem." I knew that feeling well myself, for it was reality that had seen me through many years at Rushkin Worldwide, and would see me through many more. Janus would be back, if he shared that trait with me, and I would be ready and waiting for him.

My mind swirled with possibilities; perhaps the man had engineered the entire situation. Having heard of Rushkin Worldwide from Drew and his bride, he figured it to be successful enough to pay a hefty sum to be rid of "vengeful spirits." That surely must be it, I thought. A confidence man, one with unique tricks up his sleeve to trap unwary persons in a web of ghosts and goblins. Poor Drew, he'd been taken and most likely taken hard.

Janus disappointed me, I admit, by not showing up by the time the business day was done and my staff had closed up their ledgers and saddled their pens. One by one, they bid me good day and shuffled out. I told my secretary, the last one to leave, to turn out the lights as I would be leaving shortly after her. She smiled, but her eyes questioned me as she left.

Alone in the darkened room I sat quietly, and, listening to the soft *tick* of settling floors and the trappings of bustling business, I felt oddly serene. This building was my home. The firm was my relative. My father, now deceased, left me in charge and I had done well by him, I thought. Nothing would take it away from me; not fire, famine or raconteurs with wild stories of mischievous ghouls and things that go bump in the night.

If Janus showed up at that moment, and I felt sure he would, I would call him out as a fraud and shut him down.

The front door creaked open and the man himself stepped in, as if bidden to do so. I rose to confront him.

"Ah, Mr. Rushkin," he said softly. "I'm glad you stayed to greet me, but I must insist you now leave. This most likely will be an arduous evening."

I sputtered then, damn me, and fought to regain my composure. I told him he was trespassing and that I'd have the law there on the double to see to him. I was utterly floored at his impertinence.

"Wait a moment," he said suddenly, and gestured to the far side of the darkened room. "Look there, quickly!"

In the corner, a shadow on the wall caught my eye. Its edges seem to blur for an instance, then solidify again. Then, to my utter amazement, it *moved*.

Slipping across the wall like a spider, the dark shape inched towards the filing cabinet that had fallen earlier and, once reaching it, seemed to twist its way inside. A feeling not unlike a cold compress spread over my face, starting at my hairline and then down to my shirt collar.

"See," hissed Janus. "They are here! This one seems relatively benign, but I will not guarantee it. You *must* leave or I cannot assure your safety!"

Collecting my wits, I turned on Janus. "You, you – you threw that shadow yourself! When you had directed my attention and I wasn't looking at you! What kind of a fool…"

I was not permitted to finish my accusation. An ashtray of heavy glass sailed across the room and shattered on the wall behind us – only Janus' swift actions saved me from being struck. The man had pulled me to one side at the very last second.

"Stop!" he roared and, whipping an object from his coat at lightning speed, he held it up like a beacon. Strange words he babbled then and another glass ashtray plunked down heavily on a desk across the room. A tragedy had been averted at that moment, I swear it.

I grasped at his sleeve, pulling his arm down to see what he held aloft. I thought at first it was a disk of some sort, but I could see that it had multiple edges like a geometric shape.

"No!" Janus bellowed, and pushed me back. "Good heavens, man! You know not what you do! No living creature may look at the face of this artifact, not even myself!"

Calming himself, he pulled me back towards the front door. Smoothing out his coat, Janus sighed mightily and then composed, spoke again.

"Rushkin, listen to me. This building is occupied by several spirits, some of them potentially hostile. They have some grounding here, but I'm unsure of its nature. I see now that you are determined to stay – so be it. I'm beginning to sense that some part of this revolves around you but again, I can't seem to divine the foundation of it. Frustrating."

My nerves had been stripped raw by that point and I felt my entire world go topsy-turvy. I was sure the man was a phony, a charlatan seeking to bilk people out of their money by staging apparitions and the like, but what I had witnessed there in the dark, well, I was left in a heightened state of confusion. Janus must have sensed that, too, for he jumped in with his damnable questions.

"Did you know your father's staff well?" he asked. "The air here is of an older vintage; the souls that occupy it must be from his time, not yours."

"Yes, yes!" I admonished him. "I told you that I grew up here in these offices...played here when I was very young...until I was old enough to understand what business was and they began to teach me..."

A creak of the floorboards off to our right brought our attention. Janus pressed on. "What was your father's relationship with his employees? How did they treat you?"

I told him that my father was mostly aloof, knowing full well the professional distance the head of a company must keep from his staff, but that they admired him and were loyal to him. As for myself, they all gave me their attention when they could, and as I said, I learned much from them. And my father.

"You don't remember any strife among them, any particular incident where any of them found displeasure in your presence or in your father for allowing you to be here with him?"

My thoughts turned to the past, that which I rarely allow myself, and I searched my memories. There were no fights, no ill feelings that I recollected, only a few stray kindnesses from some of the employees. My father's secretary always seemed to have a smile for me, and perhaps a piece of candy...

A small framed picture tipped over onto a desktop just then, shaking me from my reverie. I flushed again at the memories the man had forced me to dig up. It was…unseemly for a businessman of my stature.

"I'm afraid I must ask you again," he said. "Though I am fully aware it caused you much consternation the last time I inquired: what of your mother and her death?"

You may think this the crux of the matter, so ardently did Janus ask me for the information, but it was a subject that was a closed door to me. I did not dwell upon it. By not dwelling upon it, it would have no bearing on my life. But, what did it truly matter at that moment to Janus?

"My mother, if you must know, sir," I said. "I was told she died in childbirth. My father refused to speak of her, past that."

Janus narrowed his eyes at the news; perhaps it had caught him off-guard. If so, he had little time to react as at that very second a coat stand sailed across the room and into his midsection. Janus spewed out air and fell backwards to the floor.

I looked up to see a shadow on the far wall that seemed to me to be of vaguely human shape. It was not my own, nor was its Janus'.

Stepping forward, I had it in mind to see if I could determine if what I witnessed was reality or some elaborate fantasy I had conjured up. A hand on my shoulder startled me and I stopped. It was Janus, apparently revived.

"Let me," he said. "It is my business."

Motioning me to once again take my place at the door, the man took out the "artifact," as he called it, and walked slowly towards the wall that harbored the shadow. He showed the object's face to the dark form and spoke something I couldn't make out. The shadow convulsed and slipped along the wall until it disappeared into the darkness.

Still holding his talisman, Janus stepped over to the door of my personal office and, reaching out, felt along the large crack in the glass there. He shook his head and muttered. He then twisted the knob and, opening the door, stepped inside. I thought to protest then, but found I didn't have the strength. Let him see what he could see in the office; he'd find only my Spartan space and not much else.

"Rushkin," he called. "Was this also your father's office in his time?"

"Yes," I croaked, utterly spent.

He nodded at that and abruptly closed the door behind him. The action caused a piece of the glass in the door to fall out and shatter on the floor. I could see then into my office, but just barely, only making out the outline of man's dark figure and little else.

Suddenly, a voice yelled out. It took me a moment to realize it was Janus'; so deep and powerful it now sounded. The language was unlike any I had ever heard in my travels, either during my education, in the service or in business. It resounded around the room and shook the building. Or at least, it seemed to.

Then, a bluish light grew in my office. At first it was only a small, soft glow, but it then expanded and soon filled the space. Through the jagged opening in the glass I could see the man gesticulating, but the light then covered him and began to seep out of the room. Accompanying it came a sound; not from Janus this time, but something wholly unearthly, a banshee's wail of growing proportions.

"Yes, you *will*!" roared Janus, and the room shook again, causing small objects to fall off the desks and a bit of fine powdery plaster to rain down from the ceiling.

The light blew out then and disappeared. Dazed, I wondered what had transpired in the office. No sound issued from it and the entire floor, the entire building in fact, was still.

Something hard pressed against my backside and I realized I was sitting on the floor, with my back against the front door. How I arrived there I had no idea. The darkness pressed in on me, thicker than before and suffocating in its nature. Fighting down panic, my eyes searched out my office and Janus. From within the depths of the office another light grew. Greenish-white rather then the blue-tinted luminance of before, it did not spread rapidly but seemed to rise up and then hover in place.

The door opened and Janus stepped through. With him came a figure.

The form was that of a smallish man, dressed in clothes more than twenty years or more out of date. He glowed from within, greenish-white and translucent. Led by Janus, the man walked – floated? – through the door and into the larger area. He did not look up. I could see a set of antique spectacles resting on his nose, which was itself bulbous. The man appeared tired and moved slowly.

"Trombley," I whispered. "Old Man Trombley. What was his first name? Austin. Austin Trombley, the accountant."

Janus looked over at me and then back to the form. I saw that he held his talisman in front of the…spirit, so as to lead him with it. I saw too that Janus made sure not to look at the object's face. The pale slip of the old man walked with Janus to a desk in the center of the room and, arriving there, it stepped into a wastebasket, one foot and then the other. The soft form looked up at Janus, questioningly. Janus smiled slightly and nodded.

"Go thee to thy rest, oh shade," he said. "Thou hast served well in life, now take thy reward…"

With that he raised one hand and brought it down on top of the old man's head. Slowly, inch by inch, Janus pushed and the glowing figure shrank down into the basket until it was gone.

Astounded, I could scarcely believe my eyes. Janus walked back over to my office and disappeared into it. Presently, he led another softly-lit figure from the room. This was a stout figure, a man of some girth but with a proud face and lively eyes. The form wore no topcoat and I could see its sleeves were rolled up and a large safety pin held one strap of its suspenders together.

"Patrick Ferguson," I announced. "Good old Fergie. The man could lift double his own weight, I swear…"

What I perceived at the time as the spirit of my father's ware-house manager walked with Janus across the room and towards me. I jumped then, not caring to be in that close of proximity to whatever it was I was witnessing, but Janus waved me to one side. He led the figure to the front door and then through it. I watched, hesitantly, as the man led his charge to the lift on the other side of the hallway.

"Go thee to thy rest, oh shade," he said as he called for the lift. "Thou hast served well in life, now take thy reward…"

The elevator doors opened and the portly figure stepped over its threshold and inside. Janus pulled the gate back across and sent it on its way. Waiting a moment, he seemed to listen for something and then turned to re-enter the offices.

Crossing back over to my own office, the man entered and within a few heartbeats exited with yet another pale figure, glowing of its own accord.

I saw that it looked like my father.

It was a tall man, stout but not fat, and broad-shouldered. He wore an impeccable suit and held what looked like a cigar in one hand. I smiled at the sight, emotion welling up in me. Could this be? And if so, how was it possible?

The man wore a calm expression on his face, almost care-free, as if a large burden had been lifted off his strong shoulders. His moustache was expertly groomed and his hair seemingly slicked with pomade. I swear I could almost smell it: ginger-apple.

Janus held his talisman out in front of the figure and the face looked down and into its surface. What it saw there, who can say? Then it looked up again and at Janus, smiled and then looked straight ahead. I watched as the spirit drifted across the room, with Janus practically in tow rather than the other way around. This was familiar to me; my father was a leader, not someone to be led. How I missed him, I realized at that moment.

The two then ended up, to my surprise, in front of the company safe. Janus gestured to the figure to continue and it approached the massive wheel and tumblers. The mechanisms turned back and forth, though I don't rightly remember the arms of the tall figure reaching out to manipulate them. Regardless, a resounding *click* was heard and the giant door of the safe swung open.

In another world, far, far away from this one, I would have been immediately alert and protesting this egregious event…but I stood silently and simply observed.

My father – was it truly my father? – stepped into the safe and once inside Janus closed the immense door and twirled the wheel and the tumblers.

I waited for the words, straining to hear them. "Go thee to thy rest, oh shade," said he, barely a whisper. "Thou hast served well in life, now take thy reward…"

Quite emptied, I staggered over to a chair and placed myself into it. Janus walked over to me and placed a light hand on my shoulder.

"There's one more, Rushkin," he said. "Let's finish this, eh?"

I feebly waved at him to continue and once more he entered my office. Why these apparitions all came from that one room I could not say at that time. It seemed odd to me, but hadn't the entire affair been nothing but one ponderous oddity?

Janus spent much more time in the office with what I hoped was truly the last one than he had with the others. When I had all but made up my mind to see what the devil he was up to – had I the energy – the door opened and Janus stepped through. No form or figure accompanied him. Curious, I stared at him but he would not turn to look at me.

Holding out a hand with the strange talisman in it, he spoke. "Come forth."

A smallish shape appeared in the doorway, as if the shadows therein had finally, reluctantly relinquished a prize. It glowed like the others and with the same hue, but it was distinctly different than the three that exited the office previously. It was a woman.

Janus stepped back to give the shade room to move forward. The figure looked to be about forty years old or so, with long hair in an elaborate braid and held by a simple pin. The dress it wore was not currently in style, but it fit well and was in good condition. In all, it was a woman who seemed sure of herself yet not demonstrative. And it had sad, very sad eyes.

"Miss Phillips," I said, more to myself than anyone. "Abigail Phillips, my father's secretary…" I searched for Janus' eyes for some sort of confirmation, but in my heart I felt sure I was correct. Pretty

Miss Phillips, with the sad eyes.

Janus began to lead the glowing figure forward and I had the presence of mind to look around me to see where I could go to stay out of their path. The man made a sound in an effort to catch my attention and I looked up at him. He shook his head once. I admit I didn't fully understand his intention at that moment.

Then, all became clear; he led the figure over to me.

Part of me, some deep inner part, wanted to recoil. This was something of a ken that far exceeded my own, and I fully recognized that. But, another part of me was transfixed by her eyes, which caught and held my own and glowed a little brighter when doing so.

Miss Phillips – I remembered then that she had never married – was a comfort to me as a boy, assuredly, and I was always glad to see here at the offices. She had passed away shortly before my father, I recalled, but from exactly what I never knew. She was always kind to me, much more so than any one else on my father's staff...perhaps even more than my father himself.

"Talk to her, Rushkin," said Janus. "Let her hear your voice."

What does one say to the presumed spirit of a person long since gone from one's life? I challenge anyone to compose their self at such a moment and speak rationally.

"Hello," I stammered. "Hello...Miss Phillips? I'm afraid I don't know what..."

The figure smiled, the corners of her eyes crinkling at the corners, just as I remembered from long ago. Then, it opened its arms and glided towards me.

"Rushkin!" hissed Janus. "Don't refuse her! Good God, man, I swear you are in no danger!"

I barely heard the man. Only the sound of rushing waves reached my ears and of such a loud cadence it drowned out all else. Then, a warmth enveloped me as I closed my eyes and braced myself. Perhaps I thought I was about to join the others in the Great Beyond.

But the warmth eventually began to fade, as did a subtle scent of lavender soap. I heard myself speak.

"Go thee to thy rest, oh shade...thou...thou hast served well in life, now take thy reward..."

And with that, she was gone.

I have looked back over this document and see that it does not paint the exact picture I wished to present. I see a somewhat foolish man who was caught up in something that perhaps he, at the time, could not see through. My intention, upon reading back through it, was to tear it up and remind myself that such a waste of time for a businessman is nearly a sin.

But, as I stated previously, I am currently an invalid and I suppose time is what I have a surfeit of. My leg continues to mend, slowly, but my mind feels sharp and clear – unlike during the events described in this record.

I feel as if I should send the doctor's bill for setting my fractured fibula to Mr. Roman Janus, the "Spirit-Breaker." I awoke after the light show in my offices to find myself on a landing in a stairwell of my firm's building. The damnable man said that after "Miss Phillips went to her rest," I ran out of the offices and dashed down the stairs with my eyes still closed. My leg was broken in the process.

He further told me that my father had sworn to always be there for his employees in life and that somehow that honorable intent transferred beyond death. The spirits only wanted to be recognized, being "stuck" within the bounds of their former workplace, yet Miss Phillips seemed overly-concerned with protecting me, for some reason. "Unfinished business," claimed Janus.

Of that person I have only to say this: I question the man's character, his morals and his sense of business. Without his smoke and mirrors in my eyes I find that I could, if pressed, most likely explain everything that he presented with solid, mortal reasoning.

I must admit, though, that for a moment I thought I had perhaps seen another…great truth before me. For a moment. But one cannot always rely on such things. Someone in my line of work must remain pragmatic and with both feet firmly on the ground.

Just yesterday, I received a note from Mr. Janus asking me to record my story for his files. He also included his bill, which, I must say, was fairly reasonable. Still, in the end, it's a bad business, this "spirit-breaking."

A very bad business, indeed.

"*After many arduous years of para-psychical research I realized how few of us are in tune with the worlds beyond the world and, in turn, completely defenseless against its more egregious injustices. Once I discovered my own abilities in this regard, that of being able not only to see the forces of the supernatural in play, but also divine solutions to their abatement, my path was set. I could no more walk away from it then I could divert the wind or change lead into gold. It is my duty, and my honor, to help those who cannot help themselves against spirits who would make our mortal lives a living hell.*"

Excerpted from "Janus Speaks!"
The Mount Airy Eagle
April 10 Edition

Chapter III
THIS UNBROKEN LOCK

I'm not sure if I'm doing this right but I'm going to give it a proper try. I got a letter in the post asking me to tell the story of what happened with Sgt. Janus and so here I am to do just that. I still can't believe whole parts of the story but I was told not to leave anything out and to tell it in my own words.

I should probably make it clear and honest by saying here that my mother, Mrs. Frances Gilhooley, is helping me write this. In fact, I'm talking and she's writing. It's not that I can't write, of course, but my mother suggested that I might remember things more clearly if I just talked and didn't have to write as thoughts came to me. Plus, she was there, too, and most likely can help me to remember all of it. I told her that was fine as long as she didn't change a lot of my words, or at least not too many.

My own name is Daniel Marion Gilhooley, but my friends call me Dam. This is how it all began:

I work as a courier for a bookshop on Thackeray Street called Chapter & Verse and it's an interesting job, to be sure. One of the shop's best customers is Sgt. Janus. He lives a fair clip outside of the city and doesn't always have the time to come down and visit the shop, so as you may have guessed he's often in need of books to be delivered to him at his home. My boss says he's the type of customer who makes a book merchant's life more exciting, him always on the lookout for what he calls "terrific tomes." I call them odd.

Anyway, I know the way to Janus House like the back of my hand, so the shop always sends me to take Sgt. Janus' books to him.

On November the 15th I took a mighty large package up to Mount Airy – I think it was probably the biggest book I'd ever seen. My shop had it wrapped in brown paper, as always, and I looked forward to seeing what it contained once I got to Janus House. Sgt. Janus often lets me linger a while and watch as he unwraps his treasures.

It's his library that I love the most. It's a wonderful room, full of the kind of things that make you want to hear the story of each and every one of them. Sgt. Janus will tell me tales of anything I ask about and I always seem to go to the soldier things, those that look like they are of war. He tells me about them, though many times he looks a bit unhappy when he does so.

"Master Dam," he said to me, sitting in that red velvet chair of his, holding the latest prize I brought him. "This book is one I've hunted for close to ten years now. A decade spent seeking it out, eager to dive into its deep waters." I certainly enjoy the way he speaks, even now, after what happened.

The title of this book, if I remember it correctly, was *Homebodies in Actuality*, or something mightily close to that. It was written in German, he said, so Sgt. Janus had to translate it for me. I asked him what the title meant. He said that it was all about spirits that haunted just houses, not anywhere else; just houses. I know the man well enough to know that he wasn't making a joke with me. That made me think of the ghost that haunts my mother's house, and I told him so.

Sgt. Janus is what they call a detective. He figures things out by looking around and putting pieces together like a puzzle. I want to write down here how he figured this one out. First, he looked at me funny, like I had said something interesting – he never looked at me like that any other time. Maybe I had never said anything interesting before.

Second, he told me to pull up a chair and sit across from him. This made me feel a bit odd, but I was game so I did what he asked. Then, he looked at me with those great, green eyes of his and began to ask me questions. Here's how it went:

Him: How do you know it is a spirit that troubles your mother's home?

Me: Well, things happen that couldn't happen otherwise, right? Things move when no one's moving them and sounds happen when no one's making them…that sort of thing.

Him: How long has your family occupied the house?

Me: Oh, for quite a long time! Since before I was born, since before my mother was born, too. Years and years.

Him: I assume you have encountered the spirit or spirits yourself. Tell me, in which part of the house do these things occur?

Me: Umm, mostly upstairs, I guess.

Him: Try to be more precise, my good man. Where upstairs? In one or more of the bedrooms?

Me: Oh, no, sir! I mean upstairs in the attic! Why, not two weeks ago my mother told me she was jumbled out of sleep late one night by the most awful racket coming from the attic – as if a man in heavy boots was walking around!

Him: Ah, now we are getting to the meat of the problem! Do you know the area well? Can you describe it for me? I feel as if it is of the utmost significance…

Me: I should know it well, sir. I was just up there not three days ago, putting a few items away for my mother – though she had me go up there in the daytime. She made a point of that.

Him: She sounds a wise woman. Again, please describe the attic in detail.

Me: Well, it's just a room, really, nothing too out-of-the-ordinary, I believe. Got its windows on three sides of the house and a door from which you enter and leave. There's the chimney stack, of course, though the fireplace's been stucked up good for all my own life. Lots of boxes and crates with all my mother's stuff in 'em, and a few pieces of furniture –

Him: Stop. Describe the furniture, please.

Me: The furniture? Just a few odds and ends, sir. A chair. No, two chairs. One's a rocker. And an old lamp that belonged to my dear old father, and a trunk and a little table that –

46

Him: Stop again. I beg your kind indulgence, young Master Gilhooley, but you say a trunk?

Me: Yes, a trunk. Been up there forever. Big thing it is, and now that I think of it, sort of a funny-looking thing. I've never tried to move it but it looks heavy enough...

Him: Has this trunk ever been opened? By that I mean, within your own memory?

Me: No, not that I know of. To look on it you'd think it's been sitting there since Moses. Oh, and there's a rusty old lock on it, too! Queer thing, now that you mention it. Never seen another one like it...

At that moment, Sgt. Janus sat back in his chair and closed his eyes. I swear to you that that chair is a part of the man somehow. I rubbed my own eyes when I thought I couldn't tell anymore where he began and the chair ended. But then suddenly, he opened his eyes, sat forward again and grabbed me by the shoulders.

"You must bring that trunk here," he said. "As soon as humanly – or inhumanly – possible."

At first I thought, how would I ever get that trunk from my mother's house up to Mount Airy? The little motorcar I use for my deliveries was too small to handle that monster, so what was I to do? But the thought of being able to have the great Sgt. Janus look into a mystery right in my own family was too good to be ignored – looking back now, I almost wish I had thought a bit harder on that. As it were, I jumped right in and perhaps I'm not the better for it.

I know a man who works for Rushkin and he loaned me a lorry and his own strong back to load that trunk. Before you could snap your fingers we had the thing on its way to Janus House – and my mother along with it.

See, and I'm not telling any tales here, my mother is the sort that likes to know what's going on. Since she's helping me write this, you know that she agrees with that. When I showed up at the house to fetch that trunk, she demanded to know what I was on about and where it was going. When I told her, well, she grabbed her hat and shawl and jumped into the lorry, saying that no property of hers was going anywhere without her and that was the final word, thank you very much. Plus, she wanted to make Sgt. Janus' acquaintance. What else could I do? She went.

So, we made our way up to Mount Airy; me, my mother and the trunk. It didn't so much as make a peep the entire way. Thank the good Lord for that much, at least, for it was a blessing compared to what happened later.

When we arrived at Janus House, we were met by the lady in black who lives there and works for the sergeant. I don't know her name, as many times as I've seen her, but I'm not afraid to say right here that she gives me that weird feeling. She's pretty enough, in her way, but something about her unsettles me. My mother warmed to her like a house on fire but again, that lady makes my hair stand on end.

"Welcome, young Master Gilhooley," she said with a slight smile. "And welcome also to Mrs. Gilhooley, we presume. You honor us with your presence."

Such flowery talk always goes over well with my mother. Me, I like plain speech. Anyway, the lady in black directed us 'round to the side and to a larger set of doors that I'd never seen before – I always went in the front. The lady then asked us to come back around to the front door and that the trunk would "be seen to." I expected Mother to balk at that, but she went along and pranced up to the porch as nice as can be.

Inside, we waited in one of the side rooms while the lady in black disappeared to fetch the sergeant. We listened to the voices and the singing far off for a while – there's always something to be heard in Janus House, I told her – and presently the man himself appeared. After introductions, he even kissed my mother's hand and asked her if she had any questions.

"Well, yes," said Mother. "Tell me, Sgt. Janus, why *do* spirits haunt the living?"

The sergeant's eyes seemed to twinkle a bit and I was quite relieved to see he took such a question in good humor.

"My dear woman," he began. "You ask for that which I have spent almost my entire life attempting to answer. No, no, I'm not offended by your question, but you must know there is no easy reply for it. But, I will try to give you an answer regardless.

"When some of our fellow human beings pass on, they do so uneasily or with much in their lives left undone or unfinished. Their energies, well, *linger*. Normally, the soul is bound to remove itself to its final destination, as the supreme will of the universe dictates, but, and here is where I must falter and stumble in my reply, for some reason certain souls cannot free themselves from the web of this mortal plane. And some...some they *choose* to stay."

My mother considered this, and then spoke. "Certainly the Lord would not allow such a thing, would He?"

"I cannot presume to know exactly what He would or would not allow, Madam," said the Sergeant, still with a twinkle. "But suffice to say that in my experience it *does* transpire and such men as myself have taken it upon ourselves to...let us say, put right this unfortunate wrong, or correct a great evil, in some cases. I hope that might begin to answer your question."

"Yes, it begins to," Mother said. "But don't think I'm a disbeliever in such things, please. I told Dam that whatever might happen with my trunk, I wanted to see it with my own eyes. Lord knows I've already seen and heard my share of odd things in my life..."

"Then, let us delve into the unknown together," replied Sgt. Janus. "And we shall see what we shall see."

We were told we would be taken in hand and reunited with our trunk. Sgt. Janus said he had to "see to certain things" and left the room. A few minutes later, the dark lady returned and asked us to follow her. I wondered why it had to be her that would see us to wherever it was we were going, but I didn't argue.

My mother and I were shown down a corridor to a door, and then through the door into another sitting room. From there we passed through room after room after room – no hallways or passages but lots of rooms, one after another. After a time, the dark lady finally guided us into a passageway and then up to a very small wooden door. My mother remarked on this and we were told that this was the "Room of Tableau."

"In this room," said the dark lady. "All the world's a stage, and all the men and women merely players. You will see many parts offered up, many roles filled but not by actors – everything you witness will be real. Or *once* was real." Then, she removed an object from underneath her pelisse and touched us both softly on each shoulder with it. My mother recognized it as St. John's Wort.

She opened the door to the room then, and I had to stoop to walk through it. Mother did not. It was dark inside and I stopped, but the lady urged me to continue and, plucking up a bit of courage, I walked inside. Mother asked if this was where her trunk was and we were told that, yes, it waited for us in the room.

What a room! Even now if I close my eyes I can see it: dark, but things still visible around us, things in shadow and lit by soft light from who know where. There were rows of seats like in a fancy theater, maybe fifty in all, and they looked old but in good repair. The walls numbered eight, if I remember correctly, were full of doors, how many I could not say. The ceiling seemed to stretch upwards and out of sight, filled with darkness and hanging over us like the shadows were built from bricks. Way up I thought I could see a chandelier, but I'm still not sure. Up above a draft was kicking around, making odd noises like the sounds when the wind rushes between buildings in the city, or maybe like the calliope at the circus. It was a bit chilly, too.

At the front of the room there was a stage, and on the stage sat our trunk. All alone it was, just sitting there with nothing around it save for more doors at the back of the stage. Oh, and there were curtains to each side of the stage, red ones that like the chairs looked old but all in one piece.

"Doors always unnerve us," said the dark lady, "for they offer choices." I didn't care much for the way she said that, but decided not to make a point of it. She told us to please sit and we did, both of us, in the front row. Tiny little candles burned along the edge of the stage from side to side, but they didn't seem to be casting much light. I found my own hands shaking as I sat down. To keep them still I sat on them.

I heard a door open and then close and when I looked around to ask the dark lady about that, she was gone. Mother and I sat there in the dark and just looked at the trunk, not knowing what else to do. We felt we daren't move or say anything. Then, we heard another door open and shut and before we knew it there on the stage next to the trunk stood Sgt. Janus. He was alone.

The man himself struck such a mighty figure at that moment, like I had never really seen him properly before; which is wrong because I've brought him more books up to the house than I care to remember. But there on that stage in that room he looked, well, *bigger* somehow.

"Your attention, please," he said, as if he were speaking to an entire crowd of people. The more I think back on it, maybe he was.

"The History of the Trunk," said Sgt. Janus.

I had Mother spell that out with big letters because I swear that's how the sergeant said it, all grave and important-sounding. Sometimes you just know when you hear people say certain things in that way. Mother must have heard it that way too because she got up from her chair and walked over to the little set of stairs that went up to the stage. Sgt. Janus held out a hand to help her up and led her to the center of the stage, right in front of the trunk. I know it's hard to believe, but a kind of light appeared and surrounded her and everything else grew darker around both the room and the stage. Not one single word was spoken by the sergeant directly to my mother on what to do – she acted like she knew what was expected of her and she did it. It was like watching a…well, bless me, a *play*.

This is what my mother said:

"I have known this trunk all my life. It belonged to my uncle, Madison John Frankwright, who was my mother's brother. He traveled a lot but visited my family when he could; my father never liked him. Said he was a shifty sort, a salesman. I liked him myself, for

51

he'd always bring me trinkets from his travels and he always had mints in his pockets, but truth be told, he sometimes was very serious and that frightened me. Anyway, he up and, well, disappeared about the time I turned nine years old or so and we never saw him again. Father said he'd run off because someone caught wise to his antics, but Mother fretted over it. The policemen claimed nothing could be done for it.

"One day, after Uncle Madison disappeared, we received his effects. A man at the door who was all official-looking told my parents that my uncle's will said his things should go to his nearest relatives and I guess that was us. There were some suitcases and other boxes…and the trunk. Father went to the city and got a copy of the will and he and Mother read it. My brothers and sisters and I were excited about it at first, thinking we were going to come into some money, but my parents said that Uncle Madison was poor and that those things we received were all that he had.

"His will referred to it as his 'Indian trunk,' and by that I presumed it came from India, looking like it did. Uncle asked that we never, ever open the trunk. I remember Father was very surprised by that and he and Mother had some words between them on that point, but Mother prevailed and said we'd honor her brother's wishes and that the whole kit and caboodle would be placed in the attic.

"I know for a fact that Father went up there a few times and tried to open that trunk. I could hear him in the middle of the night, clinking and clanking around, fooling with the lock, but as far as I know he never got it open. He lost interest in it before long and my family just forgot about poor old Uncle Madison's things up there in the attic. They have sat there undisturbed now for over fifty years, but I must confess that I never thought of the trunk and our noisy ghosts in the same breath. That old house seems to have always been shifting and thumping and moaning…I guess I liked to think it was Mother and Father come back to visit me from the beyond."

Mother stood there for a moment after she was done talking, all quiet and still. I remembered some of the story of Great Uncle

Madison but never heard it all together like that. It gave me pause. I didn't know what to think. I turned to gaze at Sgt. Janus, who was now sitting next to me, and saw that he was looking up at my mother on the stage with an odd expression on his face. He then got up and offered a hand to help Mother down. She returned to her seat and he took her place on the stage. That weird light was now around him and the shadows in the room seemed to not like it much.

"The Examination of the Lock," said Sgt. Janus.

He turned and knelt down on one knee before the trunk and reached out to hold its lock. Funny thing, but before that moment I feel like I had never really *looked* at that trunk – it seemed strange to me, though I had seen it many times as a boy and brought it to Janus House myself! It was very large, maybe six feet long and tall, maybe a good three feet tall and it was black. Oh, it was a very deep, dark black, like coal or something that was pulled down out of the night sky instead of deep in the earth. It had a peculiar design to it, if you looked very close at it; sort of a series of lines in weird patterns and such. When I looked at it in that room, it was as if I had never seen it before. It...*filled* the stage.

The lock on it was a monstrous thing. This is what Sgt. Janus said about it:

"This lock is a very strange one. I have seen drawings of such a lock but this is my first encounter with one in the flesh. It is very, very old. Its weight far exceeds its actual substance – it is *psychically* heavy. I would not be at all surprised if it were partially ectoplasmic. Yes, very old and very ominous.

"You see these markings here? They are runes of an incredibly ancient nature, most likely Abyssinian or possibly even Atlantean. They give off a biting cold to my touch; they would probably not feel so to yourselves but I am sensitive to these sorts of things. Suffice to say, they are runes of warning. The lock's wards are just that: to contain, to hold, to *incarcerate*. I do not care for this lock. It is far older than the trunk itself, by many centuries, perhaps even millennia."

I looked more closely at the lock in Sgt. Janus' hand and where I

53

once thought it was black like the trunk I could now see that it was a very dark bronze, or maybe even iron. It seemed to change with every glance I gave it. I couldn't see any "runes" or whatever Sgt. Janus was going on about – it looked to be a plain lock with only a keyhole to break up its broad face.

Then, there was a rumbling. It came from all over the room.

"This trunk, this lock," began Sgt. Janus. "They do not wish to be opened by any living thing save their owner, and I am told that their owner is most likely deceased. A vexing proposition, but I think not an insurmountable one. There are stories that lie within which need to be told, and the only way that will happen is if this unbroken lock is broken."

Sgt. Janus stood and turned to face us. "The Breaking of the Lock," he said.

The man walked over to one of the doors at the side of the stage and opened it. I was, of course, eager to look inside, but I don't seem to remember now what was behind that door. Funny, that. Anyway, Sgt. Janus returned front and center with a book. I half-wondered if it was one that I had brought him over the last few years.

He set the book on top of the trunk and opened it to a page somewhere in its middle. There was a bright flash that almost blinded us but it went away as quick as it came. I heard the sergeant mutter, "Of course, of course," and he then knelt once again in front of the lock. I guessed he was reading from the book because he'd glance at it and then at the lock and then back to the book. He did this several times.

Then, the most amazing thing I had ever seen up to that moment in my life happened. Sgt. Janus bowed his head and then his whole body had a sort of conniption, a fit that rolled through him. He opened his mouth after that strange movement and out came a silvery thread! Mother saw it too because I heard her gasp and start, but for some reason I put my hand on her as if to tell her everything was fine.

The silvery strand came out of his mouth like thread off a spool

54

and it moved forward like a snake, becoming thicker and thicker. It *glowed*, I swear! When it was as thick as rope – it might have even been corded like rope – the whole thing inched its way down to the old lock on that trunk. It reached out like a little child, real hesitant-like, and the silvery rope touched the lock.

I tried to see if Sgt. Janus was watching what was happening, but I could see he had his eyes closed; the thing that came out of his mouth was moving of its own accord! Its end splintered into several strands and those surrounded the lock and spread over it. When that happened, it looked to me like the lock grew darker and even shrank back a bit from the strands. Then, the silvery cord gripped the lock tight and, at that very moment, Sgt. Janus' whole frame jerked and I thought I heard a low moan come from him. His eyelids flickered but he kept them closed.

What happened next we have decided together, Mother and I, to call a *battle*. It's the only thing it could be called. There were no swords or guns or yelling and screaming but a part of the sergeant went forth and made war with that lock. It grew darker and darker in that room and Mother and I held onto each other for dear life and I'm not ashamed to say we were very frightened. At that moment, all I wanted was to take Mother out of there and the trunk be damned. Sgt. Janus could keep it.

Then, after long minutes, light seemed to creep back to the stage. The room seemed calmer. The silver cord that stretched from Sgt. Janus' mouth to the lock...it seemed to blow away like a cobweb in the wind, or a like a dream. Yes, like a dream. When it was gone, the sergeant called out in a loud voice something that sounded like "Enoch!" and clapped his hands once, very loudly. It was like thunder. And then, I swear, the lock fell off the trunk.

The sergeant stood up. We began to stand, too, to ask him if he was all right but he waved us off and straightened his jacket and cleared his head.

"The First Story," said Sgt. Janus.

He left the stage and stood an arm's length from my mother, but did not sit. He was at attention, like a soldier. With his military-style outfit, he would not have looked out-of-place at an army camp. Looking up at the stage, he called out.

"Come forth!"

The room darkened again and my mother and I leaned in closer to each other and clutched hands. The temperature dropped and it grew very chilly. I swear I could almost see my breath. Then, there was a soft glow around the trunk and the lid began to open.

Oh, God, when I see it now in my mind's eye it gives me the shakes. The lid of the trunk opened slightly with a creak and then more and more until it was opened all the way. I didn't want to see what was inside, just didn't want to see it. Mother began praying.

We could see movement in the trunk. Then, *fingers* appeared from inside which ran along the edge of the trunk and then became a whole hand. Sickly it was, pale and skinny, with awkward-looking bones, and it waved around feebly as if someone was drowning inside the trunk. The arm the hand was attached to also looked sickly, like it barely had any meat on it.

"Come forth," said the sergeant again, but more softly that time. "Come and tell your story, spirit. Here is a stage on which to tell it."

A head and a body came out of the trunk. It was a girl. She was dressed in rags and I could see that once her hair was dark and so were her eyes but now she was entirely pale like as the moon, and glowed like the moon, too. This is what Sgt. Janus said as the shade of the girl stood up from the trunk and wavered back and forth like a young tree in the wind:

"You lived long ago, but you are not certain of when. Your family was poor and you were not educated outside your simple home. Perhaps…perhaps it was around 1690? Yes, that sounds about right to your ears. You were Egyptian, and you were a curious sort, always looking around to see the world, or at least that which you could see in your village. You liked to visit the market with your mother and your brothers, and you liked to touch everything. But you never stole. Oh, yes, you never stole. You were proud of that. There was a shop that you admired, a shop of leather goods and the like. A place where among many other wonderful things they made trunks…"

The shade of the girl flinched just then, and she wavered even more. I could see right through her. Her dead eyes blinked and blinked and she tried to put her arms up in front of her but could not, I guess. Oh, the cold that came off of her! Like a winter wind, all icy and bitter.

"The man who worked at the shop," Sgt. Janus continued. "He was a quiet one, always working and he seemed only to speak to those who bought something from his shop. When you crept in to look at his goods, he took no notice of you, or so you thought. Then, he killed you.

"You came around one day by yourself, curious and inquisitive, and hoping to smell the leathers and the tools and the hustle and bustle of business. The man again took no notice of you until the moment you peered behind the curtain over the door to his back room and he clubbed you over the head with a heavy leather cudgel. You…you didn't die right away. No, bless you child, you did not die right way."

The girl writhed in the trunk, as if she was reliving something that had once happened to her. Oh, the tears fell from my eyes and I could hear my mother sobbing as if she was far off in another room. I looked at Sgt. Janus and he stood still as a stone statue.

"After he…had his way with you, he put your broken, bleeding body in the trunk. The trunk that he had made only days before, one that he had crafted with an eye towards keeping things in its depths. And you, dear girl, were the first thing he kept in it. Your body is long gone but your spirit remains, bound to the trunk and the monster who made it." A horrible sadness came over the girl's face and her hands dropped slowly to her sides. Then, she faded away.

My mother and I sat there, silently, for a long time. Finally, Sgt. Janus spoke. "Obviously, the trunk is Egyptian, not Indian as your uncle thought, but I –"

"Can't you do something for her?" wailed my mother suddenly, cutting off the Sergeant. She had said what I was thinking and I could feel the blood boiling in me. I wanted to hurt someone, preferably a trunkmaker or leatherworker.

"My dear woman," said Sgt, Janus. "Hers is only one tale within the trunk. I do not look upon her tragedy unkindly but in order for me to help her, we must continue. All the trunk's secrets must be revealed. I could no more help her now than I could hold back the rain. We must continue."

With barely enough time to catch our breath, Sgt. Janus took the stage and announced, "The Second Story."

Rejoining us in our seats, he once again called for a spirit to "come forth."

A greenish mist came up out of the trunk and swirled above it. I thought I could see hands within it but I wasn't sure. It seemed to me as if the mist was trying to form into something but wasn't able to do so, at first a hand and then an eye and then a whole head, but it continued to look like a smoky mist. It also smelled like garlic and, of all things, roses.

"The nation of Turkey," said the sergeant. "Spirit, quell your movements and unspool your tale."

The mist slowed its mass and then hung there above the trunk, like a greasy cloud or sponge. It made me a bit queasy in my stomach, and Mother, too. It also seemed like it was trying to suck up all the light in the room.

"You were a Turk, from a hilly province. You received the trunk in the year of 1736, a gift from a fellow businessman with whom you often traded goods. Your own line of work was unimportant, just things that you moved from here to there – the money was what was important to you. When you were young, you were a good lad, always helpful to your mother and father and willing to learn and to respect others. Something happened, though, when you were fifteen…you were kidnapped.

"A smuggler who was hiding himself in your town wanted an errand boy and he commanded his thugs to steal one for him. You happened to pass by the smuggler's hiding hole on the way to fetch something for your father and you were waylaid into a life of crime and debauchery. Somehow, you survived. Then, as an adult, you made your own 'business' with the blessings of your former master and you set out on a path that would bring you everything you ever wished for.

"Though you did try to conduct an honest business at first, the lure of illicit bounty clouded your mind and you delved deep into ill-gotten gains. Then…hold."

Sgt. Janus paused. A look of confusion came over his face. He raised a hand and pointed at the mist above the trunk.

"If you are trapped in the trunk, it is a situation of your own making!" he screamed. "There is someone else within! Someone you are attempting to hide from our eyes and ears! Begone, oh Turk, and let he whom you hide come forth!"

The greasy mist blew apart as if blown by a bellows. Then, a small figure stood up from the depths of the trunk. It was a young man, looking to be about my own age. He was once handsome, I could plainly see, but he was now a pale shadow of his former self.

"You were the victim of the Turk," said Sgt. Janus solemnly. "He robbed you of everything you owned, even…even your young wife, the dearest thing you possessed. He sold her to another man. He ruined you and left you with nothing but the clothes on your back. When you went to confront him, he spat on you and laughed at your accusations. Desperate, destitute and utterly alone in the world you broke down and, throwing yourself on top of his trunk, sobbed out a plea for justice. The Turk left and one of his men came in and beat you until you were dead. Your blood is now part of the trunk."

I could hear the man's sobbing right then and there, but I realized it was coming from my mother. She cried and cried and asked God why such a thing should happen.

The sergeant sprung up just then. "Wait," he said. "The story accelerates. Another shade cries out and demands to be heard. I am sorry, my dear spirit, but justice will be addressed once we hear all the tales the trunk has to tell."

The host of the young man who'd lost his wife faded from view, like a memory. I wasn't even sure if it had happened at all, that we had seen him and heard his sad story. We barely had time to collect our wits when Sgt. Janus spoke again. This time, he didn't mount the stage but remained with us in the front row.

"The Third Story," he said, quietly.

To our surprise, the trunk closed itself! Then, as we were scratching our head over that, it opened again and a sparkling shimmer of dust came from within. Even Sgt. Janus seemed a bit surprised by this, but he kept his place and watched.

Out from the trunk came the blast of a trumpet and the ghostly rustle of what sounded like curtains. The form of a man appeared, short and fat and sporting a monocle and a cape. He opened his mouth and from within it came the sound of ghostly wailing, crying and sobbing as if it sprung from a hundred mouths. I cringed at it – it stung the skin of my face like little needles and I was afraid for my eyes.

"Quiet, spirit," said the sergeant. "Relate your story and we will listen. That is our promise. You say…that you were a simple man who had inherited some land in Brussels and were returning to your native Paris after surveying the land to tie up loose ends there. You were excited by the move, looking forward to a new life in a new place and the friends you would make in Brussels. France was very dear to you but you were never the sort to stay in one place forever. You returned to Paris in 1802. There, you died.

"A traveling show attracted your eye one evening as you were packing and, noting that the posters proclaimed one of the troupe's port-of-calls was Brussels, you went down to chat with them. Part of the show included a medicine man, who offered all sorts of wondrous tinctures and potions…from his trunk.

"Yes, yes; I will hurry along, sir. You are an impatient man, I can tell. The charlatan doctor held up many cures for many ailments, and one of them was for the gout, from which you suffered mightily. The doctor noticed your fine watch and money purse and enticed you to buy some of his potion – you believed him and his claims, as did hundreds before you. You did not wait to return home to drink the potion; you tried it then and there, as the show was ending and the troupe began to pack. You, sir, ended there, too. You drank and something went horribly wrong.

"In horrible, wracking pain, pain far worse than you had ever experienced, you crawled to the charlatan doctor and gasped out your call for aid. There, in the privacy of his tent, he bid you to bend over his open trunk and he would apply a treatment he called 'acupuncture' and take away your pain. He instead took away your life with the lid of the trunk by smashing it repeatedly down on your head and neck, and then he took away your fine watch and purse. The troupe left that night and your body was not found for another week, hidden as it was by the charlatan doctor."

The man's spirit began to cry. Ghostly tears rolled down his pale face for the life stolen from him. Then, to my amazement, he stepped out of the trunk and looked like he was going to try and walk away from it. He faded as he took a few steps and was soon gone – but I could still hear his wailing.

I felt drained of all life myself. Mother didn't stir, but hung her head and shook it from side to side, muttering under her breath. Sgt. Janus moved over to her and whispered in her ear.

"It is now your turn, my dear lady. You must finish the story."

I didn't understand what he meant. The poor old woman had just seen horrors like no one ever had and she was weak from it – did he think she could even stand or speak? I was about to say just that when Mother stood up.

"You are right, sir," she said to Sgt. Janus. "I can finish this. But Dam needs to help me."

Taking my hand, she led me up onto the stage and over to the trunk. It was like walking through ice water to get there. Mother seemed to be in a trance and I thought perhaps Sgt. Janus had done that to her, but he simply waited in the front row and watched us.

I looked down into the trunk. Here was something that had caused us a world or trouble, from bumps and thumps in the night to supposed spirits trapped within it. It was more than a man such as myself could credit. I don't know where I got the energy to finish the thing but, finish it we did.

Inside the trunk was a book, a small thing, like a journal or a diary of a sort. My mother leaned down and reaching into the trunk picked it up. She then handed it to me.

"Oh, Dam," she said to me. "I can't go on, I'm afraid. I'm all weak and so very tired. Could you, son, do this? Could you tell the tale?" And then she turned away without waiting for an answer and returned to her seat. I held the little book to my chest, which at the moment seemed like the thing to do. Images came to my mind then, pictures of things and sounds. I knew what the story was and who it belonged to.

"The Fourth and Final Story," I said.

"Your name is Madison John Frankwright," I heard myself say. "You bought the trunk in 1850, got it from some place in London for a steal. It looked old but it was in good repair and you thought you could use it to haul around your goods. You took it home and it was then that you realized that it didn't come with a key for the lock. Oh, how you cursed and grumbled!

"You stuck it away in an unused room and three nights later you heard sounds coming from the room. When you went to see what all the commotion was, you saw that the lock was off and the trunk was open. You couldn't light a candle in that room, though, to save your soul. A wind kept blowing it out, but it didn't matter as the trunk provided its own light. Then, it told you its stories.

"They drove you mad. So much anger and woe and murder and sorrow – it was more than you could bear. You tried to keep it under wraps, tried to push it to the back of your mind but it was bad for your work, and soon you were not working at all and your life was a shambles. The trunk would not leave you alone and you could not seem to be rid of it. Finally, you did the only thing you felt you could do. You locked up the trunk and your house and you walked through the woods for days and then you shot yourself dead.

"No one ever found you and you insured that all the spirits within the trunk would continue to be trapped there. They had asked you, in their way, to free them and you, in your way, refused."

So, you see, the final spirit in the trunk was my great uncle. I suppose he didn't have the will to hold up to the spirits' request and he took his own life so as to not have to make a decision of what to do about it. After seeing for myself what was in the trunk, I don't know whether or not I can blame him for that.

Sgt. Janus took us aside, my Mother and I, and this is what he said to us:

"You two must make a monumental decision at this juncture. A crossroads is before you and as the last links in this unfortunate chain, you must choose the direction. There are several spirits held fast in this infernal trunk, made all the more insidious by that ancient lock. Its spells of containment are of a nature that cannot easily be broken – I do not know from where the trunkmaker got that lock but I do know its hold on the spirits can only be broken by someone with a pure heart and a strong one at that.

"You must act as judges, jury, and even executioners, my dear Gilhooleys. Your uncle has unfortunately left it to you, by way of his will, and as his family the decision falls to you. I cannot release them myself. There are good spirits herein and bad, all webbed up in the evil inaugurated by its maker. You must either free them all...or none. There is no other path."

He then let us be and we turned to look at each other. My mother is a kindly soul, which I know well, and she has led a good life. I suppose I have, too. We both thought about the little girl, the young husband and the man with the gout. We also thought of the Turk and the charlatan doctor...and our uncle. Madison was, well, maybe not a pure, good-hearted man but not an evil one, either. But he did cause a lot of trouble by not freeing the spirits and now his fate and that of the other spirits was in our hands. I looked into my mother's eyes and she into mine for quite a long time, both of us making sure the other agreed. The answer was not an easy one; still, we knew what to do. My mother turned to Sgt. Janus and asked, "How do we do it?"

He looked at us both in turn, and announced to the room, "The Freeing of the Spirits." Then, he turned back to us and with a small smile said, "You already have."

63

When the thing was done, the sergeant kept the trunk, now empty, and the lock, now useless. He said their destruction would be a "long and arduous process" but that he'd see to it. We thanked him and, very, very tired, we left the Room of Tableau and Janus House and, with my uncle's diary, returned to the city. The book has already begun to answer many of our questions.

My mother's house is very quiet now, which is kind of a nice thing, I suppose. She has a good deal more room in her attic now, too. That came in handy when just the other day, she accepted the surprise delivery of a brand new trunk.

It was with the compliments of Sgt. Janus.

ABOUT TOWN WITH YOURS TRULY

A promise was made two days ago here that Yours Truly would spill forth with more salacious details of the New Year's Eve soiree at the Craig Ballroom, above and beyond those of the more mundane variety previously related. Here is that promise delivered, Dear Readers:

Yours Truly, attending deliciously incognito in a borrowed chapeau and garters, witnessed one of Mount Airy's most popular and, shall we say, bohemian couples, not in a lover's clench, but in the throes of a decidedly wicked tiff. Such a row! A smattering of its clattering could be heard clear out into the dining room and into the sitting parlors; one wonders what could have brought about such a brouhaha. Mr. K.L. has recently come into quite a neat and tidy sum and Mrs. N.P. does have quite an unruly appetite for dresses and shoes and...oh, Dear Readers, please remember that Yours Truly never said the couple were married. To each other, that is.

And then was spotted, or perhaps glimpsed, Mount Airy's favorite eccentric and recluse, S.R.J., a man who is only spoken of in hushed whispers and, quite often, nervous titters. Brrr... Yours Truly can still feel the chills even now on her lily-white arms while this missive is being written. Anyway, a stunningly remarkable thing occurred at the soiree concerning the handsome uniformed gentleman: he was seen dancing. And not just dancing, but with an exceedingly lovely girl, the two of them all alone on a semi-private balcony where one could still hear the music – but, fortunately, not the stirrings of war from K.L. and N.P.

Our normally-taciturn S.R.J. seemed quite entranced by the girl, she who was fitted out in a gloriously glowing gown of what appeared to be white silk. In addition, the girl's nigh-translucent skin and mesmerizing platinum blonde locks suited her gown to a "t" and her matching gloves and shoes were also immaculately appropriate to her ensemble. Yours Truly would go so far as to say she was nothing short of a vision, and S.R.J. would seem to have agreed at that moment. But, here is a troublesome coda to this story: Yours Truly cannot tell you Dear Readers what name this vision answers to, for that little fact remains a mystery. Inquiries were made, questions asked, but, after many blank faces and even blanker memories, not a stitch was uncovered, regrettably. In truth, the girl seems to have disappeared after the Witching Hour, leaving our poor S.R.J. out in the cold, forlorn and...dare we say it...lovelorn?

Oh, it troubles Yours Truly greatly that the girl could not be identified for your edification, Dear Readers. Why, it was almost as if she wasn't there at all. You don't suppose...?

Before we become even sillier, let us end this installment and promise to meet again here for more news from high society.

Ta!

From *The Mount Airy Eagle*
Tuesday, January 3rd

Chapter IV
LYDIA'S LOVER

It is Christmas Day and I do not feel like celebrating, so a request that I set down a record of recent events in my life comes at an opportune time, as I am in a mood to reflect on the past as I transition to the next stage. Everyone I know or have known has left me, so there shall be no gifts, no Christmas toasts, no holly and mistletoe and no caroling this holiday season.

This I set down partially as a record of the last days of Edouard Reinhart, my friend and my lover. He is dead. The other part of it concerns myself, Lydia Levallois. This is our story, such as it is, and I tell it as if you knew no part of it at all.

Oh, I see now that to write of our love, Edouard's and mine, is a potentially foolish thing indeed. Anything I could possibly set down, any words that I would choose to express that love would sound hollow to anyone reading them save ourselves. I am well-read and I know the truth in this: to read of another's romance without truly knowing the two people involved, knowing their *souls*, you cannot fully appreciate the depth of feeling between them. Already I am certain I am expressing myself poorly on this point, but suffice to say – we were in love.

Edouard and I were inseparable from the moment we met until the moment of his death. We ate every meal together, read books together, went out together into the world as a single whole. What interested him interested me, and vice versa. It became so that often times we would finish each other's sentences. Yes, we lost friends by the droves. We did not care; we had each other.

The Levallois are a wealthy family; I do not care to try and obscure this fact. I was well-schooled and pampered as a child and I most likely broke my parents' hearts when I "took up" with Edoaurd. You see, he was of a family from what my father charmingly referred to as "the other side of the tracks." Edoaurd, while not poor, was simple people from a simple place. It did not matter to me, or to him that I was of wealth and comfort.

As I have said, are interests were shared and we would quite often fall into fits of obsession over various subjects such as, oh, 18th century romantic plays or lawn bowling or even jazz; we flitted from one to another, always having a marvelous time with each and then moving on to the next when the previous obsession waned. Edoaurd was, you see, prone to bouts of melancholy – I too now find myself a victim of the same illness.

One of our shared interests was in the occult. I mention this because it was one of the very last subjects we meditated over and it also hangs over the following record like a shroud. Our investigation of the supernatural was a superficial thing then; I see that now, but presently it occupies my every waking thought, and many of my dreams.

Together, Edouard and I laughed at the table tippers and the séance box crowd, saying as how they delved into a pool with depths they could not begin to discern as a child pails sand on the beach to create a fragile little castle. We fancied ourselves students of the great Houdini, two fearless detectives exposing charlatans and seeking out the real truth behind the game of life and death. I must admit, Edouard took it a bit more seriously than I did, though.

Bored one evening and completely sated after a delicious meal, we set up a board and amused ourselves with several rounds of rousing the spirit world. I can still hear Edouard's deep-throated laughter as we set about contacting a spinster great-aunt of his, a sour lady who had died a few years past and left a worthless estate behind. I reveled in his joyous sounds that night and loved him even more for them, if that were possible.

Then, something frightened him. I wish I could say exactly what it was that suddenly overtook him and made him pause as he worked the glass, but I do not know. Not for certain. I think he *saw* something, for I remember his eyes growing wide and the smile fading from his perfect lips and the color leaking out of his countenance. He insisted we put the board away and for days after he sulked in a dark funk.

At first I told myself it was nothing much more than the melancholy which periodically overcame him and decided that I would not allow it to affect my own superior mood. But, when two people are so in love, so intertwined with one another, one cannot for long ignore the suffering of the other.

I remember very clearly the day that my heart could take little more of his long face and emotionless speech and I made the trip into the city to visit our favorite booksellers, Chapter & Verse. There, I traded several tomes of the supernatural and occult for a quite beautiful and very old set of the complete works of Shakespeare, with an eye towards convincing Edouard that together we would read every one of the Bard's plays and then act them out.

I entered Edouard's apartments later that day to find him dead.

It was his heart, the doctors said, though Edouard had never spoken to me of any such condition concerning it; I wonder sometimes if he knew of it at all. One physician told me that his heart was weak from the day he was born and that there was nothing he could have done about it had he known. It was, as he said, "only a matter of time" before it failed him.

For myself, it was as if the universe itself had failed him – failed *us*. Yes, it was as if God Himself had taken my love from me. I was inconsolable. I ranted and railed at everyone and everything, the Creator most of all and I spoke horrid things aloud. To say I was angry would be a high degree of understatement; I was livid with grief and disbelief.

Why should such a loving, caring young man be stricken down in the prime of his life, and leave behind a woman who adored him more than anything on this Earth? Where was the sense in that? What did it matter to God if Edouard went on living and loving?

Why not take some other person, some hapless wretch whom no one would miss if the Deity was thirsty for blood? I was sure there was no justice, no righteousness left in the world and I was not afraid to shout it to the heavens.

Shock led to anger, anger to violence, and violence to a complete disregard for myself and for others. For weeks, they tell me, I did not eat, did not bathe, did not read, did nothing at all that Edouard and I would do together. I was half a person. I damned everyone who came near, just to be certain I'd get whoever was responsible for stealing my love away.

His family told me that his funeral was very nice, though simple, of course. I did not attend. No looks of piety or sympathy did I need at that time. Edouard, dear sweet Edouard, would have understood.

That was in October. Some time later, I stood up, washed my face and decided to continue to live. Then, four weeks ago, on November the 28th, Edouard came to me.

I was preparing for bed that evening, still feeling numb after Edouard's death but not so angry as before. Life had settled down to a dull roar and I simply lived it, nothing more. My little house outside the city is a quaint thing, an old family holding in need of a caretaker and positioned just far enough from prying eyes to suit me. Edouard loved it. One day we thought we'd live in it together once we were married.

That night was a clear, quiet one. The dinner dishes had been cleared and after a bath I was brushing out my hair when I heard an odd noise. Living alone out in the country, I had long ago identified and cataloged every sound that my house and its surroundings made, but this was something peculiar to me. It sounded like a bird had gotten into the attic.

I sat there in my bedroom listening to the faint sound, transfixed by it, a kind of fluttering of, well, wings I suppose. It waxed and waned, as if the creature had been trapped and was trying repeatedly to escape, until finally, after about a half-hour of it, the sound faded away. My ears strained to hear if it was still there, but after several minutes I reasoned that the poor thing had found the way it had originally entered and had freed itself.

Then, there came a great crashing sound. My heart beat furiously and I wondered at whatever it could be to have made that loud of a cacophony. The attic is a tiny space and I keep very little in it, and nothing much that could have fallen over and made such a crash. Quickly, I finished with my hair and dove into my bed, pulled the blankets up tight to my chin and shut my eyes.

As I lay there in the now-silent house, I began to sort out my thoughts. As Edouard is almost constantly on my mind, I reasoned that it was very possible, most assuredly possible, that my love himself was trying to contact me. Once the thought occurred to me, a warmth spread over my entire body from head to toe and I was quite certain – no, absolutely certain – that Edouard had made his first foray back to the waking world…and to me.

The next day I felt happy, a feeling that I thought to have abandoned me. What a marvel it was, to know that love endures beyond the grave and that two conjoined souls would never truly be apart. If anyone could ever have made such a journey, it would be my Edouard. I felt pity for anyone who had lost their heart's best friend and perhaps ignored the signs of contact. I would be henceforth cognizant of such signs.

Three days later, I was sitting at home worrying over a few pages of a rather scandalous novel that has recently been making its rounds when again I heard an odd sound. I set my book down quietly and held my breath; did I dare hope? As I listened, I heard the distinct tread of footsteps in the next room, growing a bit stronger with each step; they seemed to be coming closer. I jumped up and ran to the door and flung it open but there was no one there, just an empty room. Chiding myself that I had imagined the footsteps – perhaps it was only snow falling off the eaves outside – I returned to my book. Soon, I fell asleep in my chair.

I do not know how long I dozed but I awakened with a start when something touched my hand.

Such a thing makes a distinct impression; when fully awakened I could still the feel the lingering sensation on my skin. I raised my hand to my face and the unique scent of ambergris came to my nose – Edouard's scent. Tears rolled down my cheeks, tears of joy. Here was more proof that he had returned. I looked around, searching for more signs in my little house of his presence, but there was nothing to be seen. Guessing that it was perhaps quite a strain on him to come through and make such a straightforward gesture, I went to prepare for bed, happy and content.

Later, while brushing out my hair, I chanced to look up into my mirror and there saw a figure across the room by my bed. Dark and misty it was, more a silhouette than anything but with faint features discernable, like highlights on an arm or a collar or a chin. I gasped and wheeled around to view it directly, but it was gone. Oh, I was sure it was Edouard! When I think of it now, there could be no doubt that the love of my life had been standing right there in the room with me.

I fell asleep content, knowing that Edouard would try even more diligently the next night to come through.

He did not come the next evening, or the one after that. I awoke on the morning after he had tried to appear in my bedroom – what else could it have been? – with a vague weight of melancholy upon me, and though I normally would have taken a walk to dispel it I did not want to leave the house. I did not want to chance missing Edouard. The day stretched out interminably as I sat and did practically nothing from dusk to dawn and went to bed that evening feeling weak and sickly. The next day was even worse. I had no signs of my love. Perhaps, I thought, he was unable to come through completely and I cried myself to sleep.

I dreaded sleep, assuming it would be fitful and restless as rotten as I felt, but amazingly I slipped into a deep slumber. It was like dipping into a cool stream, one we all seek as it flows through our fevered nights; here it was and it was like a balm for my troubled soul. I should have known it was also a herald for the sweetness that was to come.

In dreamland, I walked through the city until I came to the door of a certain set of apartments. Barefoot yet not a bit cold, I knocked on the door though in the waking world I had never done so, always entering of my own volition, but it was not so overly odd to me. No one came to answer the door, so I opened it and entered the flat; it was the rooms I knew so well, just as I remembered them. Here were all of my love's things, all arranged as he liked and all now so sadly without their owner. I went around and touched each one in turn.

Something told me then that I was being watched. I turned to see who it might have been, my heart hoping for only one answer to the question. There was the sense that someone had just been looking through a doorway and then disappeared from it, so I followed. With each room I entered, the same sense prevailed; someone had just exited. I walked through room after room, hallway after hallway, the apartments impossibly large and sprawling. Each time I approached a different area, there was a fleeting glimpse, a sense that someone had just turned the corner. My speed increased as I began to trot than run from room to room, hoping that whoever was leading me on the chase would be just ahead of me and I would catch them up. I began to laugh, for the hunt was a merry one and I looked forward to capturing my delicious prey. Oh, I remember what fun it was!

The last room approached, finally, and upon entering it I realized it was my love's bedroom. There, in the corner, was a lovely lacquered screen that I myself had bought in an engaging little shop of Oriental curiosities I once stumbled upon in the city. I sensed someone was behind it; in fact, I could just make out the very top of a head of hair above the screen.

A voice came from behind the images of Chinese dragons and quaint little children – which all seemed to be moving – and asked me to pause a moment. I did so, smiling from ear to ear, and the voice asked me to describe the person behind the screen. That I could not see beyond its edges did not seem to bother me in the slightest, for I knew whom it was that I wished to describe. In a sort of queer rhyming couplet, I detailed a young man of twenty-two years, lustrous black locks and the skin tone of a city dweller, tall and somewhat gangly in ill-fitting clothes and piercing eyes of blue that while the color of a babbling brook sometimes glowed with warmth when they looked upon me.

The voice smiled – I could almost see it – and seemingly satisfied with my recitation asked me to name the young man behind the screen. Though the game was all-together a charming one I stamped my little foot and called out Edouard's name in mock-exasperation; let him appear, I demanded!

Edouard, my dear, sweet love stepped out from behind the screen and into my arms.

I cried and cried and we danced and danced; oh, the music was all of my favorite tunes rolled into one. He asked me to pick one of his own favorites and when I did it played sweetly and we danced some more. Edouard was warm to the touch – oh, so warm as if life and vitality flowed through him. The next I knew, we were sitting on the floor facing each other and smiling with the grins of fools in love.

Edouard asked me what I wanted to do and thinking a moment I picked a favorite word game of his. Back and forth we tested each other and then he asked me to talk about one of his most especially favorite painters; I choose Degas and reminded him of the exhibit we saw together a few years ago and the works there he treasured the most. Edouard then asked me to tell him how his family was getting on and to name each one, but at that I drew the line and insisted I would not; he pondered that for a few seconds and then smiled and laughed and calling me a little minx wished me a good day.

Then, I awoke in my bed, the morning sun streaming into my room and the scent of ambergris all around me.

The melancholy returned and along with it an overwhelming desire to be with Edouard. The sensation of holding him in my arms was a real one, and somehow I knew that it was more than a dream – he had actually visited me. It seemed more real with every minute I thought about it.

I dragged myself out from under my covers and throwing on some clothes and arranging my hair decided my moroseness would lift if I could view some of the places Edouard and I used to frequent, so I returned to the city for a tour. Walking its streets and breathing in its many smells, I felt my spirits lifting somewhat but not entirely so. It was quite a long time before it dawned upon me that one of the sources of my melancholy was that it was Sunday.

Allow me to explain: my family is one that lays claim to being a Christian one, though that is more in pretense than in practice or deed. As I was growing up, my siblings and I were dutifully marched to church on every Lord's Day and subjected to all the pomp and circumstance that made up the mass. I dreaded it. Oh, please do not think me wicked, but when one is forced to do a thing without sufficient explanation of its merits and in fact quite a bit of brow-beating and threatening, well, one rebels. To this day, I cannot face a Sunday with anything other than loathing.

Saying that, I found myself on that particular Sunday, just a few weeks ago, not only attempting to throw off my depression but calmly walking up the front steps to our church. Upon entering I looked around, selected a pew in the back and sat. It was several minutes later that I realized I had arrived between services.

I got up to leave but heard my name being called; it was the parish priest, a nice old man for whom I had always felt sorry but had never been sure of exactly why. He walked up to me with his hand extended and a smile on his face and remarked that it had been a long while since he'd last seen me. There was no reason for me to be unkind to the man and I admitted that yes, it had been a long time. Standing there, talking with him, gazing at his priestly vestments as he rambled about this and that, a feeling of need came over me. Before I knew it, the priest and I were sitting on a small bench outside the church that overlooked the little cemetery that it bordered. I was calm then, so very calm.

Something in the way he looked and the way he spoke filled me with a desire to open up to him when he asked about how I had been getting on since Edouard's...since he'd been gone. The priest's eyes were warm and caring and I began to tell him of the visitations.

Oh, it was a joy to tell someone that my love had not been extinguished but had now in truth been rekindled. I told the priest of Edouard's first charming attempts at contact and then, feeling not bold but altogether very comfortable, I told him of my dream – which of course, was not a dream.

The priest he – I can scarce write the words – he recoiled from me in horror.

He in no uncertain terms told me that there were no such things as ghosts or spirits in the Lord's great plan and that once we died there was no returning; the immortal soul went on and did not revisit our mortal plane. To believe in such a thing was near-blasphemous, he said. Oh, how his hackles rose!

I in turn told him that I was quite certain that there were more things in Heaven and Earth than he had ever dreamt of in his quaint philosophy. How could love, the greatest universal force known to mankind, the underpinning of God's grand design, ever die? Surely that would be a cruel trick for the Creator to play on his loyal subjects, and I told the priest as much. He shook his wizened head and looked at me with widened eyes and that which I hate most of all: pity.

He reached out and grabbed my arms as if to shake me and pleaded with me to come to my sense; there were no spirits of the dead haunting the living, he shouted, only *devils*.

The little priest spat out the word like a curse. I lingered in the air as he stared silently at me, breathing hard from near-hysteria – I thought that he might have been stricken with apoplexy. I removed his hands from my shoulders, stood up and brushing down my skirts I thanked him and walked away. If he said anything further I did not hear it.

The next chapter of my tale is a difficult one. That which came even later gives me some food for strength to tell this part in full, but still it chills me to my core to even think about it. I will soldier on – an apt phrase, as my story will reveal.

It would be some days before I came out of the sulk that followed on the heels of my encounter with the narrow-minded priest. I do not wish to say anything more about him save that if he is a representative of the current state of the clergy, we are all doomed.

At the beginning of last week I received an invitation for a party to be thrown by one of my last friends on Earth, as near all others had deserted me. Edouard and I went to few parties and more recently I had attended none at all; it was not the sort of atmosphere that I enjoyed. You see, I relished having Edouard all to myself, a state of mind that anyone in love should recognize. Something took hold of me, though, as I read the invitation and in place of my normal reflex to toss it in the wastebasket, I responded to it saying I would be happy to attend. Woodenly, I picked out a gown suitable for a Holiday soiree when the day had arrived and arranged a sort of a rictus of a smile on my face; I would be congenial at the very least, if not outright friendly.

Once at the party, I soon found myself growing numb and tired after only an hour or so. Oh, my friend's house is a marvel, almost a palace actually, and decorated for Christmas it was a twinkling gem of candles and holly and gaudily-wrapped presents – but it did not serve to interest me. Everyone there told me I looked beautiful but I felt more a painted doll, hollow inside. My weariness finally overcame me and ascending the grand staircase to the bedrooms I found a private spot to rest myself for more merrymaking to come.

I find it more than troublesome to continue. But I will. It must be told – it is part of the story.

I lay down on a gigantic bed and stared at its canopy for what seemed to be quite a long time before the sounds of the party below faded and sleep came. It was a sound sleep, at least at first. Then, as I slumbered, strange sensations made themselves known.

At first there was a cool breeze and I remember shivering. Following that came a breath of warm air that settled on my feet. I could feel my shoes being removed, slowly, one by one and then a luxurious heat was applied to them. Oh, it was magnificent...the sensation wound itself between my toes and around my heels but never enough pressure to tickle them. I could hear myself making small sounds of appreciation. Then, the heat, now growing in intensity moved onto my legs. Oh, I must stop for a moment...

This blanket of sultriness wrapped itself around me, beginning with my feet and legs and then extending to my entire body. I did not wake, or at least I do not believe I did, though I was seemingly aware of all that was happening to me. At some point I heard myself say Edouard's name...yes, I am sure of it. When I did so, the heat increased and lay upon me like a thick downy covering. It...touched me. It slid over my arms and my neck and lifted my hair from the pillow. I was certain it was my love, certain, certain...my ears prickled as my name came to them like a summer breeze, all humid and laden with desire.

He touched me in intimate places. I...could feel my skirts being lifted and displaced and then something like soft kisses fell upon me, marking a path from the nape of my neck just below one ear to the tops of my breasts over the plunging neckline of my gown... then lower...and again...under my skirts...and...oh, it had to be Edouard! It must have been Edouard!

I state plainly here and forever that Edouard and I had never been intimate with each other. We talked of it, perhaps solely in a light manner and we were aware of each other's bodies but it was, by unspoken mutual decision, something that could wait. By withholding from that supreme sacrifice to desire we thought it would be all the more sweet when we finally succumbed to such pleasure.

But, there in that room, I was wrapped not only in the flames of a kind of passion but also of mounting confusion – Edouard and I were lovers in all but the sharing of flesh! How could this be happening? I writhed and clutched but no man was present there that I could discern. Oh, it was maddening!

I screamed. It had gone too far and I fled from it like a scared child from the dark. Scrambling away, I ran from the room and down the stairs. I felt only panic, nerve-jangling panic, and flight was the only sensation I craved at that moment. I ran out the door and onto the veranda, barefooted and disheveled, with what I am sure was a crazed look in my eyes.

I then ran headlong into the arms of the most amazing man.

Heart pounding in my breast and barely able to catch my breath, I was caught from falling over the veranda's railing by a dark and handsome stranger. Practically carrying me then into the light that shone from the house, the man asked me if I was all right. Flushing profusely, I assured him that I was and that I had had a small fright.

He asked me then to describe to him what kind of fright I encountered. Feeling foolish, I could only assure him that I had recovered and he needn't pay me any mind. He insisted I sit for a moment with him until he could be assured that I was indeed well. I looked into his green eyes and acceded to his wishes.

He was a tallish specimen with sandy blonde locks and a clean-shaven face. It was a good face, though somewhat hard and with what my father would have called a "professional" look about him. After we sat down at a cozy little table off to one side of the veranda and just out of the scope of the revelers' droning buzz, I noticed he was a military man of a kind. His dress was formal, like that of a soldier's and of that cut, but without any rank or insignia adorning it. Almost forgetting my ordeal in the bedroom, I was enraptured by this man's charisma. He introduced himself as Sgt. Roman Janus.

We talked, at first the kind of trivial little talk of two people who've just met – I began to realize he was attempting to put me at ease and, frankly, doing a splendid job of it. Roman's voice was deep but with a honey tone to it that made it so wonderful to listen to. We talked and then he asked me what had frightened me so.

I chose to tell him instead that I had recently lost someone very dear to me and that I was not used to being alone. He nodded solemnly as if in understanding, perhaps even commiseration. Then, I was sure of it because, quite intriguingly, he told me a story.

It seems that in his younger days – I could not for the life of me guess at how old Roman was in the present – he loved a girl with all his heart and soul and she led him a merry chase until finally returning his love in full. Her name was Nocturne, and he was sure she was the one with whom he'd spend the rest of his life – but then an accident occurred which robbed him of his love. Nocturne was struck by a sled one wintry evening while they were out skating and she died in his arms before help could arrive. Roman looked very sad as he told me of her, but all together composed and dignified. It made me think of Edouard.

When he had finished I found that my hand had come to rest on his arm, as if to communicate the great depth of common feeling that I had for his loss. Then, hesitantly, gauging each look that I could discern on his handsome face, I told Roman how Edouard had crossed the great barrier between life and death and returned to me. I implored him with my eyes to believe me. Placing his strong hand on mine, he told me that not only did he believe me but that he had made it his life's work to believe in such things.

I reminded him that he had asked what had frightened me. He nodded. I began then to tell him of what had happened upstairs – I felt I could confide in him after he had gifted me with his tale – and he asked quite emphatically if I felt I had been accosted by one of the guests. I assured him that was not the case. There was a sudden charge in the air and Roman stood up so suddenly that his chair toppled backwards and over.

In a commanding voice, low but forceful, he demanded that I lead him to the room in question – immediately and with all haste.

Through the doors and up the grand staircase we flew, paying no mind to the startled looks from the other guests. At the top of the stairs he urged me to point the way so I led him to the bedroom in which I'd slumbered and once there he stepped in front of me and placed his palm flat on the door. Roman lowered his head and closed his eyes, almost as if praying or meditating, and mumbled something under his breath, the words of which I could not make out. The tension in the air soared.

He then flung open the door and together we peered into the darkened room beyond. It was as I left it, with bedclothes in disarray and my shoes on the floor by the bed. There also appeared to be a fine mist in the room, a queer thing so fine as to almost be invisible, like waves of heat on a hot day. Then, the mist *receded* into one corner of the room with a kind of popping sound, like a sudden displacement of air. My every nerve stood on end.

Roman strode into the room and approached its center. Looking around, he studiously scrutinized every inch of the room; what he was looking for I do not know. The mist had all but disappeared. Fascinated despite my growing terror, I walked into the room to be closer to Roman and with a booming crash the door slammed shut behind me.

Roman wheeled around to look first at me and then at the door. A look of resignation passed over his countenance, soon followed by one of cool determination. He beckoned me closer and when I had stepped over to him he warned me to stay as close to him as possible but to stay out of the way of his arms and hands. Before I could barely nod in abeyance I was flung suddenly and violently onto the bed by some unseen force.

A voice spoke; it was Edouard's, but deeper and strange. At first it was in an entirely odd, guttural language that I was not familiar with, and then in English he complimented Roman on bringing me to him. Then, he laughed. It echoed around the room. Roman ordered the voice to release me, that I wasn't to be man-handled.

The next moments were ones of sheer horror; the force which held me down began to crawl all over my body! As the mocking laughter continued, I felt rough hands crushing me, lifting my skirts and my legs and pulling at my hair – the bodice of my dress was rent in two and something that felt like claws tore at my chemise – oh God, oh God! It was horrible…

A roaring like the rushing of great waters came to my ears and the room began to spin as a prickly, burning heat spread over me. With all my strength I tried to free my limbs from the force and lift myself off the bed, but to no avail. Then, I heard Roman yell to me – he told me to look away, look away, look away! I exerted myself mightily and freeing an arm flung it over my already-aching eyes. There was an incredible flash of white-hot, searing light and I felt I was falling down a deep, deep well…I cried out to Roman to please not hurt Edouard…I screamed…I screamed…dear God, please don't let him hurt Edouard, not when he was so close, oh, so close to me. Why should it be that Edouard must go away again? What had I done? What had I done so horribly, horribly wrong to be punished in this way?

Then, as swiftly as I had been trapped, I was released. The fiery heat was gone. The room was as still as the tomb and dark. I lifted my head to see a shaft of light from the slightly open door where stood Roman whispering to someone on the other side. After a moment, he shut the door and turned to me. I rushed into his arms and wept.

Roman helped me over to a chair and there sat me down in it. I noticed that he had put something away in a pocket of his jacket; I said so aloud to him. He told me that I needn't bother myself over it – suffice to say it was something that helped save the day.

When I had been given some water to soothe my parched throat – I felt as if I was sunburned all over, too – and Roman had placed his jacket over my shoulders to cover my tattered dress, with quivering voice I demanded that he tell me what had happened. He knelt in front of me and made his explanations. He made me look him square in the eye, oh, those beautiful green eyes, and told me that what I had encountered was most definitely not my Edouard.

I shook all over. A palsy shook me and for several long minutes it held me in its grasp, like the force which had held me to the bed. When it passed, I found Roman had been holding me, rocking me like a baby. Still soothing me, he explained that sometimes an entity that so very much seemed like one of our dearly departed loved ones would make contact with the living. These he called *infernal spirits*. They were not the souls of human dead but wandering vagabonds whose only reasons for existence were to spread evil and in doing so ensnare innocent souls…like my own.

My Edouard, he explained, was not my Edouard. I had been lucky, he said, very lucky to have escaped with my life and sanity.

Roman admitted then that he was more familiar with confronting the spirits of the dead than foul things from the pit, but what he had attempted was enough to dispel the entity that had chose to emulate my love. It should never bother me again.

Oh, how I wept. I wept for what I had lost. I wept from sheer exhaustion. Roman held me for a long time, until I had no more tears in me to weep. I had been through a terrible trial that most mortals could never bear, he said, and that I should be proud of my unflagging courage in the face of such an evil – and that I was not to be ashamed for being fooled. Wiser people than myself had also been fooled and paid for it with everything they possessed, body and soul.

I asked him what he had told the person at the door, and taking my chin in his hand he smiled mischievously and said he'd told our inquisitive hosts that I'd imbibed a bit too much of the bubbly and needed some time to myself. I smiled back at that.

Much later, he arranged to see me to my little house and before we parted Roman asked me how I felt. I looked at him and told him I felt quite well, thank you very much. I felt as if a great weight had been lifted off me and that I thought perhaps I could look out from under the darkness and finally see the light. I thanked him and returned his jacket.

He left me with the knowledge that I understood what had happened and that Edouard had moved on to a much, much better place.

I do not who will read this record. I suppose it does not really matter. I am happy to have been asked to set down this record, regardless of who will actually read it and why. Once I have finished it I will dutifully post it to the return address.

Outside, it has begun to snow and I look forward to walking out into that lovely carpet of Christmas white. It is so peaceful and serene. It will make for a beautiful coda to my story.

Edouard came to me last night. He told me that he was sorry that he wasn't able to warn me of the evil thing that had taken his form and wreaked such havoc. Tears ran down his face as he told me how sorry he was. I kissed his hot tears away and told him of how much I missed him and that I forgave him. I knew that all along he was watching over me, somehow, even when I was in my most dire of peril. He took my hands in his and told me he couldn't go on one more minute without me. He wanted me, *needed* me so much.

So, I am going to join him.

Whoever reads this record first – perhaps it will be my friend Roman – will also be the first to know that I have gone to be with my love. In a few minutes, I will walk a ways into the forest and he will be waiting for me there and we will be together forever.

The priest was wrong. Roman was wrong. Love never dies. And evil can never stand in its way.

Be well.

"I will be able to tell you precious little of my service to my country while in uniform. You see, the file on my entire military career has been sealed for the past several years and is accessible only by those at the highest levels of both the service and the government. I myself am bound by law to not divulge any details that may be found in it, including those of which you inquire.

"Above and beyond that, the final days of my service were marked by personal tragedy, a private matter of which I am sure you would understand and sympathize with my reluctance to speak of it. Suffice to say that I was given an honorable discharge and I look back on the bulk of my service with honor and pride. I also hold no ill will towards any of my fellows or superiors. If you wish to pursue the question further, though I beg of you not to, you may contact Col. Drew Montaine at Fort Temper and address the matter to him. Perhaps he may be able to offer you that which I cannot."

Excerpted from "Janus Speaks!"
The Mount Airy Eagle
April 10 Edition

Chapter V
THE CORKWORTH FORTUNE

This tale has its twists and turns and not a few rude awakenings, but overall I dare say it will read like a dreary mess – especially if I'm to be its teller. Still, I shall endeavor to do as requested and provide a "record" of the events over which my dear friend Sgt. Janus so ably presided, seeing as I have time on my hands. I promise to also provide the necessary play-acting and make-believe that those who'll read my manuscript are unaware of the events herein. I'm told that's what the teeming millions before me have done - how wizard!

This, dear reader, is a murder mystery, the solution to which surprised even myself. It began quietly and rather pedestrian…with fisticuffs.

We all convened one blustery early March evening at Janus House to…oh, I suppose I should introduce our cast of characters, what? Well, I shall be a bit mischievous and have them take their bows as we go along; I *am* the storyteller here! Let's see, yes: we all gathered for a weekend at the house of Sgt. Roman Janus, as we have done many times in the past, and prepared ourselves for repasts without peer, slumber and solitude without equal and the most scintillating of conversation. Well, the first two at the very least.

I, Holden Muir, arrived second, as is my custom. I find he who arrives first often catches one's host in the throws of feverish preparation and it tends to sour the entire weekend – a look behind the curtain is not always so engaging. I believe it was Tristan LaPlante who had unfortunately arrived first on that particular date. Regardless, I threw down my bags and asked where Corkworth might be;

one needed to know where that man was at all times. Nobody knew. So be it, said I.

Arturo arrived third – that is Arturo Colapietro, Italy's magnanimous gift to the women of the world, of course. Then, as a tardy fourth came Mr. Francis Shell, lawmaker and doombringer. Hail, hail! The gang was almost all there!

We four chatted among ourselves, patiently waiting on both our host and the other spoke on the wheel of chums to show their bright faces. We are a relatively amiable lot; that is, when Corkworth is not present. When he is among us, there are not so much pleasantries as there are skirmishes. In fact, there was one such brewing at that very moment of heel-cooling in the grand entranceway to Janus House.

The man in question finally stomped through the door and hostilities broke out almost immediately. Well, I must admit that perhaps I played a very small part in that, Lord love me.

"Ho, Corkworth!" I offered. "I say, had you found a better party?"

The little man scowled, a permanent condition, and ignoring me marched up to LaPlante. Letting loose his bags to fall nearly upon the poor man's feet, Corkworth snorted and cocked his little head.

"You're a liar and a cheat, LaPlante," he purred, and Tristy, bless the boy, took a swing at him.

Let me explain, if I may, that Mr. Tristan LaPlante had obvious little love for Mr. Bertram Corkworth. In fact, why, bless me! All of us present were of like mind on that subject! Being a rather rum sort, Corkworth has that sort of effect on people; if you were to look "boorish" up in yon dictionary, there you would find a portrait of ol' Berty.

Arturo's beef with Corkworth went back many years; something over a woman, if I recollect properly. That's certainly no surprise, of course, considering the hot Italian blood that flows through the veins of the mighty Signor Colapietro – but Berty? One could scarcely credit him with intimately knowing a woman than one could flap their arms and float gently to yon silvery moon! No, it still amazes me to this moment the tenor and timber of the argument between those two.

Mr. Francis Shell is a politician of some renown, I'm told; I myself never bother with such things. Absolute power corrupts absolutely, I always say – ask anyone. Shell's earned quite a reputation in his district for winning every time he should lose and greasing the wheels of government for all who've dipped into their own pockets for him to do so. Corkworth, filthy rich as he is, fancies himself a budding political candidate and, well, politicians hate rivals. Never, ever raise the topics of taxes and tariffs between them, I beg you.

Tristy? Well, that's a strange one, I must admit. I've never been too sure what exactly characterizes the tiff between him and our pudgy pal; suffice to say it tends to become venomous between them whenever they are together and neither one eating or sleeping at the time. Such a puzzlement!

Me? What shapes my own disdain for Corkworth? Why, only the most important thing upon the surface of this wide world – we are business competitors. That, and the filthy lucre he has gained from his enterprises, of which he is always quick to remind us poor rustics. We both toiled in the business of exotic comestibles and sundries, but, yes, some of us toiled more than others. Need I say more? I thought not. Onward and upward! You are wondering where the goblins and ghouls in this little story lurk and you shall have them anon…

Now, you may also remember a scuffle betwixt LaPlante and Corkworth, yes? Well, into that mêlée, at that very precise moment, strode the towering figure of Sgt. Janus.

"My friends, please," said our host, somewhat emphatically. "There is a rack of lamb simmering for us patiently, and I shouldn't wish to keep it waiting. Can the match be reconvened after dinner?" He took in the scene: Arturo standing off to one side, teeth gritted and his fists clenching and unclenching; Shell impassive with his dull face but very aware, and Tristy and Berty circling each other like pugilists. Our host spread his hands in a gesture of peace.

And with that, the battle ceased. I don't know *how* he does it. Never ceases to amaze even myself.

Here was my good friend, Sgt. Roman Janus, come down from upstairs like Zeus with his thunderbolts and suddenly we were all his obedient children. He ushered us into dinner and we trotted along, quiet as church mice. While the meal was served and then when we tucked into the wonderful feast, I took the opportunity to covertly examine my old friend.

Janus and I served together, long ago, he as my sergeant and I as his toady, and had been companions ever since. I saved his life once, you know, though we never speak of it. Funny that; you would think it would come up in conversation now and again, but my friend seemed to have put it in the past to stay. Those days in uniform were a carrousel of utter boredom punctuated with moments of sheer terror, you understand, and some men are keen to lock it all away – queer, though, that Janus had retained his rank and military-style dress into civilian life. I can't fathom it.

Have I mentioned his profession these days? Oh, dear me; *there* is a subject! The sergeant purports to be a ghost hunter of a kind, a seeker of spirits and spooks – I would scarce credit it, but, alas that particular evening proved to be a lesson that no one then present shall ever forget, myself included. Prior to that fateful night, our little group had perhaps humored Janus in his pursuits, raised an eyebrow at a particularly ghastly story of his mayhap, but I am sure that the whole of us went home only half-believing his tales of "spirit-breaking." I mean to say, in this modern world of ours? No, it was difficult to credit it…then.

As I studied my friend at the table, I noted the thick sheen of melancholy that hung on him, like the fog on the moors. The others may not have noticed, but I spent time in foxholes with the man and we learned to recognize each other's moods and catalog them. This was a rare one indeed for Janus. I had heard he was quite shagged out over a recent case of his involving a young suicide, a girl who, bless me, it was said had touched his heart. The wonders of this wide world are a perpetual source of amazement; the sergeant had never looked so grey to me, or so listless. I pondered the meaning of it all…

I was shaken out of my reverie by a crowing from Corkworth over some sort of entrepreneurial sally of his and its rewards. His fortune, it seems, continued to grow by leaps and bounds and...oh, have I mentioned Fetters yet? Ah, please forgive me, dear readers, for I have failed to introduce a rather important, as it turned out, member of our cast: Mr. Darwin Fetters, Mr. Corkworth's personal secretary.

Firstly, I mean *really*; a secretary? Are we men or are we *prima donnas* to be coddled? I enjoy being waited on as much as anyone, perhaps even more so, but the pretension and extravagance of a personal secretary, my word! Chalk one up for Corkworth on that sorry score. Anyway, his lackey, Fetters, was a quiet sort who always hung in the background and was perpetually nervous. I usually ignored him as looking at him most always made me queasy; his stammering and shuffling were enough to depress anyone. I had also noticed that the man had been looking rather threadbare of late, and failed to even meet one's eyes when being spoken to. An all-together odd bird. Alas, I should not speak ill of him I suppose. He was simply going about his job, the sorry little fool.

Now, where was I? Oh, yes! There we were, all together and happily digesting a splendid meal, when our host decided to supply us with a story for dessert instead of, say, a nice pudding or some other dainties. This is simply Janus' way and we had long ago given up on trying to change him. I will attempt to recreate the story he told that night herein:

"There was a case," he began, as he always began each story. "Where I was called to a charming home not far from here that was experiencing all manner of occult disturbances. When I arrived, at the behest of the lady of the house, I discovered very nearly all the symptoms of what the Germans call a *poltergeist*, or, quite literally, a noisy ghost. As I began my investigation it soon became evident that I was to receive no help in any form from the family, so I ventured into the quagmire of the dwelling's ether with almost no foreknowledge of the problem's history. Sadly, the spirit that haunted the structure was revealed to be that of a young lady of twenty years or so – at the time of her death. It was all I could do to coax her out into the open, all the while avoiding one thrown brick-a-brack after another, but ultimately I prevailed and hunkered down to the business of determining the root of the troubles: the girl was unhappy over the circumstances of her demise. It seems she was a pretty thing in life, a flower in young womanhood whose presence attracted every strapping young male in the county...but there was someone who could not bring himself to share her with the world. Someone who begged her not to stray too far from home, who was suspicious of her every movement and expression and who, in the end, could not stand to see her growing up and look forward to a life of her own. Her own father, as it turned out, the man who reared her, had also murdered her. He fancied if he could not keep her and hold her close, then no one would. The family knew nothing of this before I arrived; it tore them to pieces. I put the sad shade to rest but for the family I could do little. It had rotted from within."

We all looked at each other once our host had finished his tale and then again at him. Confusion reigned; it was evident on everyone's faces.

"Well," I ventured. "On that quite cheery little note, I think I shall be off to sweet slumber and pleasant dreams!" And with that I stood up and prepared to make my exit.

Shell nodded and wiping his mouth and taking one last swig of the fruit of the vine, bowed humbly and mumbled his *bonsoir*. Arturo rolled his eyes and, mumbling to himself in Italian, stalked away from the table. That left only Janus, Corkworth and his secretary and Tristan LaPlante. Tristy stared solemnly at old Berty for quite a long moment, but then he too ascended to his bed.

Amazingly, Corkworth walked off with Janus, beckoning Fetters to follow. Yes, I wondered at that. I had suspected for a goodly amount of time that our rotund friend was, well, *conspiring* with our host somehow...oh, if I must say *consulting*, then I must, though I don't care much for it. Something altogether untoward was going on between them and it sat poorly with me. Rumor was that Corkworth owed his considerable fortune to the advice of Janus, although in what fashion, I cannot say for certain. Was the good sergeant raising the freshly and filthy rich dead to whisper investment advice in Corkworth's ear? The mind boggles!

The very thought hurt my head. My own business struggled while…ah well. If wishes were fishes and all that rot. I shan't wish to sound so soundly rum, you know. And petty. I am many, many things – and have been called a few things, too – but I will not stand for being called petty. I observed Corkworth lean into Janus as they walked away and gesticulate as he regaled the man with heaven-knows-what sort of sallies and rejoinders. Let them keep their own council, said I. The man could afford to be an ass, I suppose.

Shrugging off the dire tale with which we were saddled and the annoying habits and confidences of Monsieur Corkworth, Esq., I made my way upstairs. Now, I am a wonderful guest and observe all the decorum that one should as a guest in another's home, but, I will admit to partaking of the particularly heady pleasures of traipsing around Janus House at night.

The house itself is a most singular structure, perhaps the most unique dwelling in the world. They say the sprawling mansion was not design and constructed as one unit, but actually assembled from several other houses. One can truly appreciate such gossip when one gazes at Janus House's façade; eclectic and varied, there are no two stretches of it that are similar. Bless me, it is the most wondrous of mansions, I dare say. To walk its halls and corridors and rooms is to fancy yourself a Cook or a Columbus – but beware! Here there be dragons!

That evening I loped through the great house, taking in its nooks and crannies, its parlors and galleries. I am sure I have only ever seen a tenth of it, oh, I am quite sure. It seems to…*change* every time I have been fortunate enough to visit my friend in his den, as if once the house had settled it would occasionally rise to find a new position and rearrange its limbs for another few months. But, I will not go on record – this record, in fact! – to say Janus House is alive. Good gracious me, no!

A terrible, horrible insomniac who would give much to be a restful, thankful somnambulist, I wandered Janus House that night with a purpose in, well, not exactly the front of what I laughingly call my mind, but most definitely its rear quarters. I worried over many things, which may give fuel to my sleeplessness, and I wished to cry out my weary soul on the shoulder of the Jewel of Janus House. You see, I sought its housekeeper.

I have heard her called many names, but whatever may be her true appellation I cannot say – oh, no; I cannot say. Do you know that I have never learned it? In all the years of claiming Sgt. Janus as my friend and intruding upon his domicile, I have never been able to wrangle from him – or anyone – the name of she who keeps his house the very image of civility and cleanliness. My powers are weakening as I grow old, perhaps. A pity.

Regardless, I came across the lady near Janus' study. She did not startle easily and when I approached, she only looked up and cocked an eyebrow.

My lady in black is a painting, all shadows and midnight secrets. Her hair is…her eyes are…ahh, me. I cannot do her justice, poetic or otherwise, with mere, mortal words. She is a creature of the imagination, a muse of night and breaker of hearts. My own measly organ she impaled like a butterfly and plucked its wings long ago.

"Mr. Muir," she cooed. "Out for your usual late-night sortie?"

"Of course, of course," I returned. "Won't you deign to join me, my dear? We could make beautiful, sweet music together as we walked these halls, eh?"

My lady does not suffer fools lightly, alas, and I am a poorer fool for it. I quickly reasoned it was only a brief chat she could afford me that evening.

"You should be getting to bed, Mr. Muir," said she. "You need your beauty rest, poor thing."

Ignoring her winning sarcasm, I grilled her for information on Janus House's other guests, but she was as closeted with her opinions as a nun in a cloister. Nothing could I glean from her, but I doted on her every sweet breath and drank in her scent. But she did end on a cryptic note:

"There are strange forces flitting about tonight, Holden. I seem to be at a loss in determining their strength…and their origin point. Please be careful, will you?"

Her honest concern, dear readers, was salve for my wounded heart, though in actuality her warning was somewhat disturbing.

"Good night," she said finally, and disappeared once again from my life.

Watching her depart so intently, I almost didn't notice Tristan LaPlante lurking about.

Old Tristy is an inveterate lurker of the highest order; little wonder he has few real friends. Thankfully, one of the other beauties of Janus House is that one may easily spy on others without being seen – but you may also not see those who spy upon you in turn. Thus was the case at that moment: LaPlante did not see me, but I most definitely saw him. And I saw who he saw.

The door to Janus' study opened just then, freeing a beam of light from inside to pierce the corridor with its jolly brightness. Corkworth exited from the room and turned to bid a sober good night to Janus himself. Berty seemed apprehensive, somehow, and perhaps not terribly keen on making the journey back to his room. Janus said something that, while I could not make out the words, sounded placating and comforting. Is that not just like him, I ask you? The man is a saint.

I made my own escape from behind a ponderous potted fern and hurried down a side corridor, one that I knew would speed me on my way to the guest wing, toot sweet.

Turning into said wing, I could hear Arturo's thunderous snoring issuing forth from his room like blasts from a wounded tuba. I am not sure why, but there was a strange quality to it, one I could not place. Hurrying along I found myself passing Corkworth's door – it seemed I had beaten him there. Outside the portal, I spied a full tray on the floor in front of it, no doubt my dark lady's handiwork, at the request of our fat friend. The man could eat like no one's business.

We only lacked the right honorable Francis Shell, I mused, for a full curtain call. He was nowhere to be seen. Alas, a politician should neither be seen nor heard, in my estimation.

Eventually snug in my bed and feeling blessedly woozy after a chapter of Wilkie Collins, I paid the ferryman to escort me over and down the River Lethe. We all awoke two hours later to hear of the murder.

Oh, you want *ghosts*, do you? Be a bit more patient with me and they should be along presently. It will be worth your wait...a most incredible tale.

The heavens had opened up sometime in the night and we were deluged. Oh, what a storm! And in its midst, a murder. How stereotypical. But, I suppose a fellow must take his place on the stage whether – or would that be weather? - or not the theatre ceiling is leaking.

Thunder crashed and boomed mightily as I was awakened to the sounds of screaming. Yes, in point of fact, I can sleep during a thunderstorm; the claps and flashes soothe me and allow the Sandman to whisk me away. Crazy, is it not? Regardless of my sleep habits, these screams infiltrated my slumber and that of the other guests. We all came a' running to see what we could see...

I wonder why it was that we all ran towards Corkworth's room, every last one of us. One of us was most assuredly a murderer, and knew that fat fool would definitely be in the middle of the action, but the others? Was there a general assumption among us that if there were high-pitched screams in the middle of a dark and stormy night, that somehow Bertram Corkworth would stand at its apex? Oh, what a delicious puzzle! There's one for the psychiatrists!

But, as we approached our dear friend's door, there was the man in question! Standing there, disheveled and discombobulated, Corkworth was howling like a wolf at the moon and, bless me, looking a bit like one, too. Shell asked him what his game was; I like a man who takes charge! The others nodded. I will list here there individual states of dress or undress, for posterity:

1. Corkworth, in pajamas, hair ablaze and mouth open in terror.
2. Shell, in dressing gown, looking like he stepped out of an advertisement for Dr. Redneck's Peaceful Sleep Tablets.
3. Signor Colapietro, half-naked, all-too hairy-chested and wielding a large ashtray, most likely pilfered from his nightstand.
4. Tristan, sartorially splendid, fully dressed as if he had never gone to bed.
5. Myself, of course, the fitful insomniac who had been enjoying, emphasis on *had*, one of the best nights of sleep he'd had in months.

About this time, you may have begun to wonder at the whereabouts of our host, Sgt. Roman Janus. Well, let me tell you that as soon as that thought reached my own fevered mind at that time, the man appeared…like a ghost. He, too, was fully dressed, but rather rumpled, I noted, as if he had eschewed bed and thrown himself into a particularly deep and perplexing volume in his study. His countenance looked odd; he spoke as he approached.

"My friends," he called. "What the deuce is going on? Bertram, please stop that infernal racket! What ever is the matter?"

Corkworth paused in his wailing and looked over to Janus, eyes wide and with a look of confusion etched in them. And terror; oh, yes, terror. The man's hand shook as he pointed through the open door to his room. He could not speak! Bertram Corkworth without something to say! I half-expected him to say that he had found a decimal point off on his balance sheet or that the state of modern banking was "such a farce," as he always reminded us. Alas, it was none of those things.

Janus led the charge as we all piled into the room and made our way towards the single light that was burning in the bathroom. There, sprawled on the tiling, mouth open and tongue swollen and extended, lay the cooling corpse of one Darwin Fetters.

From that surreal moment on, events flowed freely and dastardly quick. There was a supreme rush of emotions and movements once we discovered Fetter's body and looking back, I see them as a jumble. I will venture to sort them out in this record.

First, the question was raised as to the secretary's state: how was it that he came to be in such a deceased fashion and why so in Corkworth's room?

Berty moaned and the words tumbled out of him. "I had settled in for the night and after some time was awakened by a flash of lightning…I got up to draw myself a glass of water and, oh dear me! There in the bathroom lay Fetters! Dead!"

Janus thrust out a finger like a javelin. "There," he shot. "The tray. Obviously, the poor boy consumed something that killed him. Look here at these stains on his lips and tongue – they match that of the remainder of the broth in this bowl…"

"He has'a been a'poisoned!" shouted Arturo, putting voice to what we all thought and one of us knew for certain.

"Who?" bellowed Corkworth. "Who would *do* such a thing? Poor Fetters! Oh, the humanity!"

I looked down at the body, and bless me; I noticed again his threadbare clothes and overall unkempt condition – that is, discounting his lack of life, of course. How strange that with an employer as wealthy as Corkworth that he should present himself as a pauper. I said as much to Berty. In return, I was rewarded with blank stares from all present.

"That tray of food!" hissed Corkworth. "It was meant for *me*! I ordered it from the kitchen – Fetters must have come along to see me for some reason and supped from that bowl!"

The realization that someone most likely standing in that room at that moment had sought that jowly jackaninny's death jumped like wildfire from person to person. It was almost comic, I dare say.

Janus leapt over to the body and bent down over it. There was a look in his eyes that, well…you are aware, naturally, of Conan Doyle's famed detective, yes? Just as Sherlock Holmes would be prone to fits of lethargy and depression when not going about his business as a "consulting detective," but would then be bursting with activity once a problem presented itself for solving, so too did such animation fill the frame of my friend the sergeant. It was quite something to behold, the situation notwithstanding.

He suddenly scooped both his hands under the dead man's body and began to lift it. "Come," he said with an air of extreme urgency. "We haven't one precious moment to lose!"

I protested, vehemently: "Janus! My word! You go too far, sir! This is crass, even for you – to think of defiling a corpse! Have a care!"

Shell, interestingly and wholly surprisingly, backed me up. "Roman, come now...you cannot, *must* not move him. The police must be summoned – professionals who will need to examine him and determine...good Lord, man! It *is* the law!"

We all know, I think, someone in our circles who believes that they are a law unto themselves. Never before had I thought of Sgt. Janus in that particular way, but I was now moved to categorize him thusly. The way he was man-handling the corpse was, to my eye, not quite kosher.

Our Italian Don Juan chimed in, too. "Wait'a just'a gosh a'darn a'minnit!" he boomed, to mimic the thunder outside. "We must'a be a'sure of who *killed* this'a po' boy first!"

Tristan said nothing, but I could see him taking copious notes behind his eyes.

"Gentlemen," said Janus, quite calmly, I must admit. "Time is of the extreme essence. This lad...err, what was his name again, Bertram?"

"Darwin Fetters!" screeched Corkworth.

"Yes, quite. Thank you. Mr. Fetters' spirit is still with us, of that I am supremely certain. I propose to hold it here on this mortal coil a bit longer and, hopefully, draw from it the name of his assassin.

"Come along, all of you."

And with that, he turned and ran from the room carrying Fetters' corpse like a sack of potatoes.

I caught up to our host as he hurried down the corridor towards the center of his mansion. Janus, among other things, is quite the athletic type; it was something of a chore to keep pace with him, though he was toting dead weight. We pulled ahead of the others.

"Janus," I began, puffing as I spoke. "Where *are* we going, old chap? If this is some sort of game…"

"We are headed to the Room of Cabinets, my dear Muir. There, I shall attempt something the likes of which I have never truly attempted before…rarely have I had need to *hold* a spirit in lieu of *dispatching* one."

"This is madness," I sputtered, reaching out to stop him.

He paused of his own accord. "No, this is a matter of *trust*, Holden," he said somberly, transfixing me with those damned icy eyes of his. "The story tonight was about trust, or the lack thereof. Trust me, old friend."

And with that, he was off again.

I slowed a bit and the other men caught up to me. I told them that we seemed to be following an asylum escapee into the fields of insanity. Corkworth snorted.

"Perhaps you can simply engage the services of another personal secretary, Berty old bean," I snorted back. "I am sure your overflowing coffers can withstand a small army of assistants, actually."

Corkworth stopped and we all stopped with him. His face was suddenly livid. I took a small step back.

"You supreme idiot!" he shouted madly. "I have no fortune! Not any more, if you must know! Its gone, all gone, you gossip-ridden fop!"

Well, that was certainly quite a surprise.

We all pulled up, eventually, to a door through which we had just witnessed Janus disappear. Out of breath like the sorry collection of old men we are, we flung open said door to spy a most amazing space behind it.

Lit by only a few candles of antique vintage, the smallish room was filled with cabinets. The foreboding articles of furniture lined the walls like coffins and were of many and varied sizes, shapes and types of woods – all of them of solid construction and featuring no glass fronts. It was deucedly chilly in the room, and I notice that I could see my breath before me and that of the others.

"Come in, gentlemen," said Janus. "And close and lock the door behind you, please."

Tristan was closest to the door and he reached over to pull it shut, looking for all the world as if by closing that portal it would be tantamount to burying us all alive. Oh, and one dead man, of course.

Ah, Fetters' corpse – well, Janus had laid it out on a table in the center of the room, and was busy with a queer apparatus of some kind. It appeared to be a sort of fencing mask adorned with a few squat glass tubes; after affixing it to the corpse's face he stood back and surveyed his work.

"Now, if I have made sufficient haste in removing the body to this room," he said, more to himself than any of us. "We may look to Fate to provide the rest of the necessary actions. And, of course, Nature herself."

The next passages you shall read, my invisible patrons, are of an incredible nature. No, that is a word most unsuitable for what transpired in that room. But, it is important to set it down for this record and I feel duty-bound to do so, as incomprehensibly inhuman and unworldly as it was. I am sure I fall far short of the mark in choosing the right verbiage.

The lights dimmed. We huddled near the door, moving closer to each other as small, frightened animals will in the face of terror. Janus stepped back over to the body and approached the head of the table. He placed one hand to hover over the mask upon its face but did not touch it.

"Darwin Fetters," he intoned. "Shorn of life, robbed of breath, taken from us all too soon. Though it is the promise of the Creator to release your spirit to its final destination, we ask that you yourself lay hold of it for a short time so as to answer our questions.

"Darwin Fetters! Do you hear me?"

The corpse sat up.

Janus stumbled back a step or two. "Animation!" he said with obvious surprise. "Manipulation of the original vessel! Most outstanding!"

Damn the man! We were witnessing things beyond human ken and he was as gleeful as a schoolboy with pie!

"Who is your murderer?" Janus asked, regaining his composure.

Then, the corpse raised one arm, slowly, and with seemingly great reluctance extended the index finger on its hand and...

Something sailed through the air and crashed into the corpse's chest, knocking it back onto the table. The body flopped there like a dead carp.

Pandemonium ensued. Voices shouted, arms flailed and tempers flared. Janus' voice carried above the din as he shouted for order.

"No, no! There *is* another way!"

Something in his tone dampened the chaos and all eyes fixed on our host. Janus was wild-eyed and visibly shaking, but he straightened his coat and demanded that no one was to move or he himself would thrash the man, *any* man, who did. His tone of command, keenly sharpened from experience on the battlefield, put us all in our places. We held fast.

The candles flared up at their own accord and Sgt. Janus stepped back over to the corpse. Leaning down, he whispered into its ear. Yes, I swear this. Then, removing an object from his coat pocket – a disc of some sort? – he held its face over the corpse's eyes, as if to make sure that the dead man clearly saw its design.

Came a thunderclap. The booming crash sent us all hurtling back against the door and the cabinets that surrounded it. For a moment, I thought the candles had been extinguished but it was only that I had closed my eyes against the sudden explosion and could not seem to open them again. Once I had pried apart my uncooperative eyelids, I saw a sight that still chills me to my very mortal soul when I call it up in my mind in the present.

A tentacle of a pale, greenish substance rose up from around the mask's edges and hung over the corpse's head. It swayed back and forth there, as if blown gently by an unseen breeze, producing a sickly light all its own which somewhat illuminated the room and cast queer shadows on its cabinets. Janus got to his feet and waved us all back, silently warning us not to interfere. I stole a glance at the others and they were most assuredly transfixed by the sight.

Suddenly, and as wickedly swift as a serpent in the grass, the tentacle dove across the room and towards one of the far cabinets. The door to that cabinet swung open and its inky insides welcomed the ghostly tube of light. Once the strange phenomenon was within, the cabinet slammed tightly shut.

The lights in the room extinguished then, plunging us all into complete and utter darkness.

"Now, then," came the disembodied voice of Sgt. Janus. "We shall have answers, I think."

It was not over, I told myself at that moment. There was more to come and it would not be an easy thing. I was correct. All credit to me.

The silence there in the dark of the Room of Cabinets was as ominous a thing as I have ever felt. I could not even hear the others breathing; I wondered to myself if Janus and I were the only ones left alive. What a situation *that* would have been!

Then, there came the creaking sound of a door. I reached out and touched the door through which we had entered the room and found it still to be securely closed. What then was this very clear sound of a door opening? It was not the door of one of the cabinets; of this I was quite sure. This was a massive portal, rusty from disuse and not maintained and I could feel the great displacement of air in the room as it swung open.

A great thud sounded as the door, wherever and whatever it was, had opened as far as it would go, apparently. I scanned the darkness for a sign, any sign that this madness would soon end.

A whisper of air lightly touched my face, fetid and laced with mold. Then came a sort of moan, almost as if from a child…I amaze myself to have perceived it like that, but that is what I remember. It chilled me. I hugged myself and then looked up to see a shape appear before my eyes.

Looking like the edges of a great doorway or vault, it materialized across the room from us; I heard the others gasp at the vision. Well, to be honest, I also heard myself inhale violently. Slowly becoming more tangible, it registered on my eyes as, yes, a massive doorway ringed in a glow not unlike that of dying embers in a fireplace. In the middle of the portal was darkness.

I peered into the bitter blackness and pressed back against a cabinet when I made out a shape there, seemingly far off in the distance. It appeared to move closer.

After what seemed to be an eternity, the shape shuffled up to the immense doorway and paused at its threshold. Glowing faintly from within, I could see it took on the form of a man.

It was Darwin Fetters.

The sound of soft weeping came to my ears just then; I know not who it was that was crying. I was sure it was not Janus, but beyond that I do not know. Perhaps it was myself – I cannot say for certain.

A cold wind came down the same dark corridor that the ghost of Fetters – what else could it have been, I ask you – had traversed. It blew around and through his diaphanous form and slapped our faces with its biting edge. Janus cleared his throat and spoke.

"Oh, shade," he said. "We thank you enduring the travails of your journey. We shall not hold you long, this I promise. We need to ask but a few questions.

"Did you see the face of your murderer?"

The spirit nodded its head slowly.

"Is that person in this room?"

Again, the spirit nodded its head.

"Who is that person?"

The ghost of Darwin Fetters passed a hand over its dead eyes, as if to wipe away a tear, and then raised it to point to the man who had murdered him.

Funny how you believe you know someone well, but the cards are then flipped and it appears you do not know them half as well as you think you did.

We were all changed by that evening at Janus House and by our time in the Room of Cabinets. Our little circle of friends was strained to the very edges of its maximum circumference and together we forged our way through life…and death. A taxing experience, what?

And do I now believe in ghosts? Well, I assure you, dear readers, that I have taken the entire subject under advisement. The evidence for them is fairly damning.

The evidence against me is of a similar infernal nature.

As I sit here in the Mount Airy gaol and write this amusing and frankly poetic record of the events in question I am pondering the supreme humor of it all.

Oh, I have no regrets about planning and attempting the murder of Bertram Corkworth, but I am sorry that little Darwin Fetters got in the way. I most certainly did not mean to kill him – for him I feel much pity! I think about the poor personal secretary and how he had gone for several months without being paid his wages and having to cover up for his employer's bad turn of fortune…

Did I tell you yet that I struggled after I was fingered? Yes, it's true! Well, they have told me I did, at least, and most especially when the policemen arrived to take me away. I don't much remember it myself, but it is nice to know that I still have bit of the old fire in my belly. As I said, you think you know someone, myself to be precise, and then they surprise you. I thought I might get away with it.

Let us see – should I relate the entire plot now, in the same vein as the master villains of the great old dramas? Yes, let's do just that.

My business as a merchant of exotic goods is, as they say, "on the ropes." Too many bad decisions, too many roads not taken and too much competition. A goodly portion of that competition came from the excrementally enormous Corkworth. So, I began to hate him in my own very logical fashion.

I grew to believe that he and my dear old pal Sgt. Janus had been conspiring together to whip up all sorts of devilishly good ways in which Corkworth could enlarge not only his own fortune but, in turn, his belly. Now, I learn that the two of them were conferring not over business *per se*, but on a pressing matter to save Berty from the poorhouse. Isn't that a lark! It seems that the fat fool approached Janus about contacting the spirit of his late mother so as to gain information from her on the whereabouts of a strongbox of stocks and bonds and other treasures that she had hidden and failed to disclose before she croaked. If found, he could continue to live the kind of life to which he'd grown accustomed.

Ah, what a joke on me. Corkworth had no fortune. Nothing at all to it for me to swoop in and pick up the pieces after he was dead and his business excised from the face of commerce.

You see, I had stumbled upon that tray as I walked through the halls of Janus House that night and realized it was as good an opportunity as any to poison the well, so to speak. But, drat it, Fetters came along and saw me fiddling with the food and questioned me about it in his meek, little manner. Smooth-talker that I am, I burbled my way through it and he entered Corkworth's rooms none the wiser. He must have come over all peckish and remembering the tray partook of it.

And a solid shot of exotic poison derived from the venom of a wee tiny African toad. Ah, the benefits of dealing in such markets.

I'm also told that while I've been cooling off in this cell that my good friend Tristan LaPlante has filed his story with his paper and it is currently plastered all over Hell's half-acre and beyond. Never knew he was after Corkworth for a dirty little tale; he got a bit more than he ever bargained for, eh? I should say so! I suppose Shell will come off looking like some kind of penny dreadful hero for "aiding in my capture" and Arturo the great lover will have another sweeping saga to seduce another poor girl out of her clothes. What a wealth of riches am I!

And then there is Sgt. Janus, my old friend and confidant. I thought he owed me something, for saving his life back in the day and being such a good and true friend throughout the years. I thought he had betrayed me somehow by taking Corkworth into his confidences. Ah, what a laugh…what a jolly joke.

By the way, it was Arturo's discarded ashtray that I threw in the Room of Cabinets. I'm trying to give up smoking, you see.

So, it's the noose for me, I'm sure. *I* would hang me, if I weren't me, of course. I suppose I deserve it, what?

Perhaps I shall meet Fetters on the other side – wouldn't that be a lark? And I must remember once I have crossed over to seek out that long, dark corridor…

I believe I have a few scores to settle.

"Your question seems to imply that I myself am a 'famous individual,' but I assure you that I have never sought out nor am interested in fame or notoriety. If anything, I am, I admit, perhaps infamous in some circles...

"Allow me to tell you a brief story, though, to answer your question. A few years ago I was asked to come to the house of a wealthy man who was, among many other things, a collector of art. I was astonished by the length and breadth of his collection and, upon seeing my interest, the man insisted that he give me a tour of the many paintings he owned. We walked past Michelangelos and Van Goghs and Cezannes and even a Degas or two, until we approached a small work at the end of one hallway. Pausing before it, the man indicated the signature on the painting. I looked closely to see that it was a Monet, one of his lesser-known achievements.

"The man then looked at me and explained that the work was the only Monet he owned and that he fervently wished to acquire more, but 'the demmed things are too demmed elusive." I told him that I was blissfully ignorant of such things and I was more interested in exactly why he had called me to his home – surely it was not to visit his art collection? He harrumphed and explained that he was quite certain that he had somehow acquired a spirit with the painting that hung before us, and that it was the lingering shade of Claude Monet himself. Before I could respond to this claim, the man urged me to contact the spirit and ask if it would not care to produce a fresh work or two for him. In other words, the art collector believed he had a line on wholly new Monets – exclusive to him and potentially worth a neat fortune.

"I told him that my profession as a Spirit-Breaker was to rid homes of ghosts, not parlay with them for a continuation of their earthly works, but the man insisted and I conceded that the exercise might prove valuable for future study. I asked to be left alone in the hallway and once my wish was granted, I asked the spirit for guidance on the matter. After several attempts, the spirit informed me that, to the contrary, he was not Claude Monet at all, but a simple painter of moderate skill who produced small works in his spare time. In life he was actually a chimney sweep, but in the afterlife, well, he had found some kind of fame...at least in the art collector's eyes. Could he possibly go on without my 'spilling the beans'?

"The lesson, here, I believe, is that fame is in the eye of the beholder.

We are all giants in our own minds, and we are also too often too easily blinded by the reputed fame of others. Still, better a famous artist in death than a simple chimney sweep in life…and my abject apologies to the real Claude Monet."

Excerpted from "Janus Speaks!"
The Mount Airy Eagle
April 10 Edition

Chapter VI
SCULPTED VELVET

NOTE: I have sought out and been given Permission by my superiors to provide a copy of this Official Report to Sgt. Roman Janus of Janus House, Mount Airy. The gentleman, or his associates, has requested a Record of the Events of April 1 and April 2, and owing to his involvement in the events, my superiors have instructed me to do so with the Compliments of the Mount Airy Police Department.

OFFICIAL REPORT of Officer James A. McPeek
Badge #4, Mount Airy Police Department

On April 1 of this year I was asked to investigate a report of Strange Activity at 11354 Tokyo Street, in the old North End. Our Department had previously received a notice of an escaped felon who had been seen in the very same neighborhood, so my Captain directed me to investigate the matter. Upon arriving at the address at approximately 3:25 in the afternoon, I found that the house in question was an old and large one, and in a Dilapidated and Abandoned state.

After surveying the property, which was overgrown with weeds and brambles, I decided to first talk to the owners of the neighboring properties and determine the nature of the Strange Activity. There was no response to my knocking at the door of 11350 Tokyo Street, so I then approached 11358 Tokyo Street. There, I was greeted by a lady who identified herself as the owner, along with her husband, and she agreed to answer my questions.

The lady, a Mrs. Chester Deutschendorf, informed me that the neighboring property and house at 11354 had not been lived in for at least twenty years and that she did not know who had owned it and who currently owned it. It was, in Her Own Words, an "eye sore" and that she hoped it might be torn down soon, as she imagined it be a home for rats and other Undesirable Creatures. I asked her if she had made the report of Strange Activity, but she assured me it was not her who did so. I thanked her for her time and departed.

As I left, I noticed a young boy at play in the front yard and stopped to talk to him. When asked about the house next door to his own, the boy informed me that it was "haunted," and that none of the other neighborhood children would go near it. I inquired as to Why He Believed the house was haunted, and was told that it was because it was "full of ghosts."

Having gained little useful information and not knowing the Whereabouts of the owners of 11350 Tokyo Street, assuming they had Reported the Strange Activity, I made my way onto the grounds of 11354. I choose to enter the property from the north end, at the back of the house, as I had determined that that was where the foliage was the least overgrown. Once I made my way through several dense areas, I approached the house. It was in a Far Worse State than I had presumed when I first saw it from the street, having little of its original paint left and almost no unbroken windows. The back door was hanging loose from its rusted hinges and looking closely I found signs that it had been very recently Disturbed. I drew my billy club and using it to further move the door aside, I entered the house.

I found myself on a small landing with stairs going down to what I presume was the Basement, and also up to what I discovered to be the kitchen. There was much Refuse lying about and many signs of Disuse throughout the areas. I immediately found the layer of dust and soot on the floor to have been recently disturbed by footprints, and, determining that they did not descend into the basement, I followed the prints Up and into the kitchen. There, I came across the remnants of a meal strewn about On The Floor. The half eaten food appeared to be no more than a day old or so.

A noise from somewhere else in the house attracted my attention and I Very Cautiously left the kitchen area to investigate the sound. Moving into the pantry and then into the dining room, I once again found the trail of footprints which went from the kitchen and into the main entrance hallway of the house. I had to step over many items such as broken furniture and the like, but was able to make my way into the center of the first floor of the structure. There, I found a large staircase descending into the middle of the hallway.

I noticed At That Moment that the house seemed Very Dark inside, though I could see that it appeared to still be light outside. I could not determine why it would not also be light inside the house as the windows were, for the most part, unobscured. Before I could determine what allowed for the Odd Phenomenon, a loud scream from the top of the staircase drew my attention to its source.

I looked up to see a man standing at the top of the stairs, staring down at me. He had a very Disheveled appearance and I immediately thought he might be a tramp. The man screamed again in a very Loud and Caustic voice and then began to run down the stairs toward me. As I guessed that he might, he then tripped on a piece of refuse and toppled down the remaining stairs and to the floor at the bottom. I leapt over the remains of what looked like a desk and went to Render Aid to the man. When I reached his side, I found him to be Conscious and still in a Highly Agitated state.

The man thrashed about on the floor like a madman and looking closer I could see that he was bleeding from a gash on his arm, which appeared to have been made by a jagged piece of wood from the broken banister. I called out to him to Cease his thrashing, but he ignored me. With much Effort, I subdued the man and secured him with my handcuffs.

In the rapidly fading light, I attempted to get a closer look at the man's face, and it was then I discovered that he was Arthur Donald Notten, the escaped felon our department Was Seeking. The man was completely resistant to my demands that he be still and looked to be very frightened of something or someone. I also noticed that he several times glanced at the area at the top of the stairs, which seemed to make him Even More agitated.

With great effort, I managed to remove Mr. Notten from the house and set him down in a relatively clear patch on the rear of the property. There, he became somewhat relaxed, but still cowered in Fear when he would look up at the house. When I was sure that the man was secure and in no position to run, I returned to the place that I had found him to continue my Search of the premises.

Once back in the house, I noted again the difference in the amount of light that existed both inside and out. Failing to discern a Reason for this, I mounted the stairs and ascended to the second floor where I found much the same situation of disuse and ill-repair that I had witnessed on the main floor. There were three bedrooms, several closets and a washroom, all of which looked Undisturbed. Then, I noticed Mr. Notten's footsteps trailing up to another door which, once opened, I could see led to an attic space.

Holding my Billy club in front of me, I slowly climbed the narrow staircase to the Floor Above. The stairs opened up into a smallish hallway that led to another door. Opening that, I found what appeared to be Another Bedroom. This room was decorated in a sculpted velvet fabric which had been used very liberally for most of the room's furnishings, including drapery, upholstery and bedding. Though in a high state of Neglect, I believed that I could see that the room was once that of a young person. I then noticed a large archway that opened into a connecting room on a wall that was not Easily Seen from my vantage point and made my way over to it.

As I walked towards the opening, I could see into the next room. Its walls, furnishings and decorations appeared to be clean and presentable, something that Did Not at all match the disrepair of the rest of the house. More sculpted velvet caught my eye in the area and this reminded me that I had seen the same fabric used in one of the bedrooms on the second floor, though not in such a Pronounced Manner such as there in the attic.

I approached the archway and when I reached it, my club bumped into something In Front of me, and then my foot. I pulled up short so as to not hit Whatever It Was with my face, but to all appearances there was nothing at all to see blocking my way. Slowly, I reached out and my hand came into contact with something Invisible.

The unseen Barrier resisted my attempt to enter the other room. I looked carefully and could see nothing, but there Was Something there blocking my path. If it was glass of some sort, it was the clearest, cleanest glass I have ever encountered. I felt along the invisible Wall with both my hands and found that it was not exactly Solid, but it was of enough substance that I could not push my hands through it. It stretched to fill the entire archway and was also Very Cold to the touch.

Then, I heard what sounded like a voice behind me. I turned around with my billy club ready to confront whoever or whatever made the sound, but there was No One to be seen in the room. I examined the area very carefully and could not determine where the voice came from, if there was one At All. When I turned to look back at the archway and the other room beyond it, the area was no longer clean and new. It was in the same rundown and abandoned Condition as that of the rest of the house. This made No Sense to me.

I also discovered that the invisible Barrier no longer impeded my crossing the threshold from one room to the other. I could see or feel no traces of whatever it was that Originally held me back from entering the area, but when I went to walk under the archway a Strange Feeling came over me, or rather, Through Me. It could only be described as a slight Electrical Shock that began in front of me and crossed through my Body and out again. After the sensation had passed, I realized that the other room was very cold, just as the barrier had been.

Looking around, I could see No Reason to continue my investigation at that time. I then decided to return directly to the station with my prisoner.

Upon returning, I handed Mr. Notten over to the officer-on-duty and was told that Captain Mumford was out and could not see me at that time. I decided to go and look up the property records for 11354 Tokyo Street while I was waited for him to return.

In the Documents Room at Town Hall, I found little of Value about the house and its grounds. All that I discovered was that the structure had been built seventy-seven years for a man named Silas Random, and that after he had died the property passed into the hands of his wife, Anna Random. Of what became of her and any other family Mr. Random left behind, there was no information. The house had sat empty for Many Years.

I walked back over to Police Headquarters and was told that my captain had returned and would see me. I related the events of my afternoon to him In Total and he in turn let me know that Mr. Notten had been interrogated while I was at Town Hall. Because of the man's high state of Agitation, no further information could be had from him, save a single phrase that he muttered repeatedly: "sculpted velvet."

Before I ended my shift for the day, Captain Mumford informed me that after Much Thought on the matter he would be calling in an Expert to aid in the investigation. At 10:00 the next morning I was to return to 11354 Tokyo Street and there meet with Sgt. Janus.

I arrived at the address at approximately 9:55 on the morning of April 2 to find that Sgt. Janus was already there, waiting in his motorcar. When he exited the vehicle, I could see that he used a cane to steady himself and overall had a Very Grey appearance. I asked him if he was ill and he assured me he was not. Together, we made Our Way to the back of the property where I had entered the day before.

I had Previously Known of Sgt. Janus from talk around the station and items in the newspapers, and had the opportunity to have met him in person at his home some three weeks ago when I and two other officers were called there to take a murder suspect into custody. Janus lists his Profession as "Spirit-Breaker."

I informed the man that I had been ordered to assist him in any way I could and that he was to be considered In Charge of the investigation. He in turn smiled and said that "such a lofty assignation" would not be necessary and that I was to act at all times as I Saw Fit.

As we made our way across the grounds, Janus told me that he and Captain Mumford were old colleagues and that my captain called him to look into the case, owing to Janus' Specialized Knowledge of "occult matters." I described to him my own Experiences in the house the day before and Janus said we would "see what we would see."

After making our way through the back door, up the stairs and into the kitchen, we soon found ourselves in the central hallway where I had First Encountered Mr. Notten. I remarked about the Low Quality of light in the house, though it was daytime outside, and this is what Janus told me:

"Yes, it is a Strange Phenomenon, but not an all-together unusual one. You see, a house such as this, or a similar type of structure, has a kind of life all its own. There is a Complicated System of energies that run through houses – think of it as a web – which is created not only by the original materials used in the dwellings' construction, but also by those who occupy them."

I pointed out that there were no occupants in the house currently, and there had not been any for Quite Some Time. Janus responded:

"Of course, of course, but if there Were occupants for a Significant Amount of time previously, they left their mark, their imprint on the web. I can already feel this house's criss-crossing of energies – and to finally answer your question about the light, the house is drawing upon the sunlight itself to renew its own energies. Because, as you say, there are no more Living Occupants from which to draw."

We then made our way up the main staircase and to the second floor. I also noticed at that time that the house was Strangely Quiet. The day before, there were small sounds of creaks and other similar noises of settling, but there were none such on that day. Janus Slowly and Methodically canvassed each of the rooms on the second floor and when he was satisfied I showed him the door to the attic.

He paused for a long moment as he looked up the narrow staircase to the attic and then turned to me, a somewhat Quizzical Look on his face. This is what he said:

"Although there is an odd element the nature of which I cannot divine, at this time I feel Very Certain that what we are experiencing here is a case of Imprinting. What I mean by that is, instead of Actual Spirits – the remaining life-forces of deceased human beings – I believe there are simply Residual Imprints on the web of the house. These are most likely what so frightened your escaped felon."

Janus then asked if he could go first up the stairs. I thought it to be Ill-advised, but that if he felt certain there was No Danger I would honor his request. I drew my billy club and we proceeded up the stairs. It was slow-going, owing to the man's use of his cane to mount the steps and the overall narrowness of the staircase itself. When we reached the top of the stairs, he paused before entering the hallway there. Janus turned to me and said:

"I assume you have noticed the Drop in temperature? This is Another Manifestation of the house's drawing on the surrounding energies. When that occurs, one of the basest signs is a distinct Cooling of the air. Do not be alarmed by it."

We walked down the short hallway and up to the door at its far end. Janus went to open it but remarked that it appeared to be locked. I assured him it was Not So the day before. He tapped the door with his cane but still it would not budge. I asked him to allow me to try opening it and once I moved past him, I first turned the knob and then set my shoulder against the door. I Exerted Pressure and finally the door opened.

The First Thing I saw in the room beyond was a woman hanging from the rafters.

She appeared to be approximately thirty-five years old and definitely no more than forty. The woman was attired in a long dress of sculpted velvet that I could see was of a Cut and Design of approximately thirty years ago. She looked as if she had been hanging there for Quite Some time, judging by the overall Poor Condition of the body, though I most certainly did not see her the previous day. The woman's eyes were open.

I believe that I exclaimed when I opened the door and saw the body, as Sgt. Janus was immediately at my shoulder and looking over it. He reached past me and Very Swiftly shut the door. I protested immediately and tried once again to open it, but he barred my way with his cane. This is what he explained to me:

"I am Sure that your Natural Tendencies to render aid or at the very least investigate are aroused, Officer McPeek, but I ask that you wait a moment and collect your wits. It is admirable, your reaction, but I assure you that in this case it is Wholly Unnecessary. There is no hanging woman. What you have just seen is an imprint, a Psychical Image that is, well, stuck if you will, in the web of the house."

I again protested, telling him I was sure of what I saw and that the matter needed to be Attended To. Janus asked me to calm myself – I do not now feel as if I was acting then in an outrageous fashion – and wait a moment before once again opening the door. I did as he requested and once I had waited for what I deemed to be a significant time, I opened the door. It did not require any Special Effort that time. I looked for the hanging woman, but she was Not To Be Found anywhere in the room.

Once we had both stepped into the bedroom, Janus asked me to describe the hanging woman to him. After I did so, he nodded and said that my description matched his own. At that time, we had No Idea of who she was or had been. We were both quite sure, though, that she was Deceased.

Sgt. Janus looked around the room and noted the profusion of sculpted velvet, and then remarked that the hanging woman wore a garment of what appeared to be the Same Material. I agreed. He also remarked that, just as I had thought the day before, that the room had belonged to a child and though everything in it was covered in Dust and Decay, nothing seemed to be disturbed. It was as if the room had been abandoned and then Preserved just as its occupant had left it.

Looking up at the rafters at the ceiling, I saw that one area of the wood there had been Slightly Worn away. We both agreed that this was where we saw the image of the hanging woman. Janus then noted a Curious Stain on the rug below the spot, and I made a note to myself to check for a record of a death in the house. While I did so, Janus began looking around the room again and soon called me over to his side.

Together, we stood in front of the archway to the adjoining room and saw that the area beyond was in the same Clean and Presentable state in which I had first viewed it on the day before. Janus reached out with his cane and extended it towards the opening. It connected with the Invisible Barrier, the same that I had discovered previously. The entire room was Very Cold now. This is what Janus then said:

"Remarkable. A perfect example of Large Scale imprinting. You see how the room beyond appears to be untouched by the ravages of time? The energies of the house are Focused in this area, most likely due to some event or events that were of Significant Emotional impact so as to forever impress this seeming timeless state on the room. And this barrier – incredible. I am familiar with such manifestations, of course, but not in such a High Degree of imperviousness. It is almost as if the house is…well, Protecting this room. But from What, exactly? Or, conversely, protecting us the viewers from…"

Janus did not finish his statement, as if his own words had triggered another thought. He suddenly took one step to his right, and then another. I was unsure of what he was doing. He then remarked that the word "viewers" had given him an Idea and that he needed to test that idea. While he began his testing, I took a moment to once again look around the child's bedroom.

Presently, Sgt. Janus called me back over to the archway and informed me that he had discovered something, In His Words, "truly amazing."

Janus pointed to a spot on the floor in front of the archway, approximately six inches from the invisible barrier, and asked me to stand on the spot. He then informed me:

"This is a very Interesting Phenomenon, Officer. It has dawned on me while I have stood here examining the scene in the room before us that we are viewing a Moment in Time, if you will. Note the sunlight coming into the area – it does not match the time of day it is presently. And, of course, there is no dust or other signs of decay present and everything in the room retains the vibrancy of color as it would have when it all was new. No, we are not seeing the present…this is the past. And look here; here is something all-together Fascinating. I believe it will be the key to our understanding of the events that led to this house's state of despair."

Janus took me by the arm and directed me to take One Step to my right, yet retain my original position and distance from the barrier. Once I had taken my New Position, the scene before me changed. He spoke again:

"This is not a true haunting, in the sense that we understand Such a Thing; this is, as I have said, an imprint. This room has retained a series of dramatic events, or scenes, that tell a tale rife with strong emotion – if you know how to view it. It took me a few tries, but I believe I have the sequence of events in their correct order. Let us watch and, yes, listen…"

The room behind us darkened, and both myself and Sgt. Janus looked back to see the light ebb away from us. It also grew colder. Turning back to look at the Other Room, I could see it grow brighter, as if we were in a theater watching a play.

A young girl of perhaps thirteen or fourteen seemed to appear out of Nowhere, but then I realized that she had come from the room in which the sergeant and I were standing. She sat down on the settee that occupied a spot along the far wall and picked up a sewing basket. From within it she drew out needle and thread and then picked up a swatch of cloth from a small table near her. It was a piece of sculpted velvet.

The girl, a redhead, smiled and looked up at us. I began to take a step back, Confused, but Janus caught my arm and silently urged me to retain my position. Then, we saw who the girl was looking at: a woman, approximately thirty to forty years-old, had entered the room, approached the girl and then sat down beside her. She

119

wore a dress of sculpted velvet; I realized we were Viewing the hanging woman.

This is what the woman said in that room:

"Well, my dear, I see you are ready to begin! Now, to work with velvet such as this takes a bit more Effort and Skill than when we work with more common materials. See how much bigger and stronger the needle is? See the Finer Quality of thread? Oh, I am so happy that you have asked me to teach you how to sew with this velvet! Together we shall make a room full of clothes and…and drapery and…oh! So many things with it! Just you and me, my dear. Would you like that?"

The young girl Nodded Vigorously and I could see that, though she was on the verge of womanhood, she loved and admired the woman very much and was devoted to her. The woman, who I Assumed to be the girl's mother – there was a resemblance – hugged the girl to her and looked over her shoulder to glance at a picture of a man in a small frame that stood on a nearby bureau. Then, the scene appeared to slow in its motion and then stand Perfectly Still.

Janus clicked his tongue and we stood there for a long moment, thinking about what we had just seen. Then, without saying a word, he directed me to take Two Steps to my left, once again retaining our same position and distance from the barrier. I felt as if there was a breeze of sorts that moved in the room behind us, but not wanting to move or Look Away from the young girl's sitting room, I was not sure of it.

I could see that the room now looked very much the same, but that there was a covering of sculpted velvet on the settee with small, matching pillows. The light seemed to me to Indicate a Time late in the afternoon or early evening.

The young girl Entered the Room much as before, but this time she was holding the hand of someone and leading them. It was a Man.

He was, I would estimate, approximately thirty years old, but I Concede that he may have been older. The man was dressed in

120

simple, rough-hewn clothes, but clean and in good repair. He was tall and wore a moustache that would have been somewhat Fashionable at a time thirty or more years ago. He was smiling at the girl, with a look of amusement on his face. She sat herself on the settee and spoke in an awkward fashion, an Obvious Attempt at sounding older and appearing to be more sophisticated than what her clothes and surroundings revealed. This is what she said to the man:

"Oh, I do declare! Why, Mr. Manatee, have you ever had such a dinner? My mother is a fine cook, is she not? I am so glad we met and we were able to provide you with a...bit of a rest stop on your Long Journey. Where was it that you said you were headed, sir?"

The man, who I now guessed to be a drifter, looked around the room and then back at the girl. He sat down beside her and leaned in close to her. I could see the girl's nostrils flare, as if she was drawing in his scent. He smiled and spoke to her:

"Anywhere and Everywhere, Miss Velma. I am a traveler of the world, bound for parts both Exotic and Sublime. Oh, the stories I could tell you...but I can see that you are a gir...woman of Good Breeding and have probably traveled extensively yourself."

The man then leaned back and Almost Completely laid himself out on the settee. He put his hands behind his head and looked up at the ceiling, but I could see he was also glancing at the girl from out of the corners of his eyes, Gauging her reactions.

"Yes, that was a Fine meal. Yes, indeed – your mother sure does know her way around a pot and a pan. Why, I bet you're Very Much her daughter in that sense. And what a fine room this is, all decorated in velvet....you know, they say that the skin Awakens at the touch of velvet. Now, is that true, Miss Velma?"

The girl blushed and tittered, Playfully Swatting at the man and looking away so as to avoid meeting his eyes. He smiled Broadly and, letting out a barking laugh, grabbed the girl's hand and began to knead it with his own. She spoke once more:

"Why, Mr. Manatee – you are the Charmer, aren't you?"

The scene froze, as it had before.

Janus then stepped back from the Barrier and I did the same. He reached up to rub his eyes and I asked him if he felt Well Enough to continue. Here is what he told me:

"I must apologize; I have been rather Fatigued of Late. Last month, I had something of a Nasty Turn and...well, this house is also very draining. Do you not feel it yourself? It is using every available bit of energy in the vicinity to show us these scenes. The air itself is Disturbed, almost as if there was Something More going on...but, come now; let us continue. This idler, this man-of-no-means is an Irksome Chap with no propriety and I sense he is at the center of the disturbance. He is the key – I am Sure of It."

Together, we took another step to the left, at Janus' direction, and looked up to see the scene shift to what Appeared to be night-time. The room before us was lit by the soft glow of candles, and a light breeze blew in from a small, open window.

The girl again entered the room. She did so in a very much Different Manner from the previous two times; she appeared shy, hesitant and nervous. I saw that the front of her dress was almost Completely Undone and that she was holding it closed over herself with one hand. With her other hand she attempted to keep her long, red hair, now Disheveled, out of her face. I also noticed small beads of perspiration on her forehead and neck. She kept her face down and turned her back to us.

Then, the man, Manatee, entered. He arrived in a gliding motion, very cocksure and With Purpose – he was bare-chested and also perspiring. Sliding up from behind the girl he put his hands on her shoulders and caressed them. Then, burying his face in her hair, he spoke to her:

"Now, Velma, don't you go and Run From Me. I can tell that you like what we've done – your eyes tell the Truth of it. This is what Can Happen between a man and a woman, and you're a woman now, so don't you turn from me now and say it isn't so. It was Fate that brought me to this town and Fate that allowed me to come and rent a room here in your mother's house – if it hadn't happened I would Never have met you. I've seen you watching me since the moment I arrived, and I've been watching you..."

122

He turned the girl around, but she tried not to look him in the eye. I could see now that her lips were Swollen and red and that she had begun to cry. She said to the man:

"Oh, Harry, don't think me such a baby, but...Mother wouldn't approve of this, I'm sure. Its not that I don't like it – I Do. When you touch me...oh, please! I'm so Confused! Before tonight, I had never kissed a man, let alone done what...what We Have Done. But, know that I would do anything, anything at all for you!"

The girl was now looking up at the man, eyes Wide and Pleading. He had turned his head from her, as if to refuse her, but now he swiveled his face back around suddenly and began to Violently Kiss the girl and paw at her dress. Then, he quickly picked the girl up in his arms and carried her Directly towards us. Forgetting Myself, I moved out of their way and they disappeared before my very eyes.

When the light in the room then began to flicker, I thought At First that it was the candles we had seen. It was not; it was the room in which we stood. Janus stepped out into the middle of the bedroom and tilted his head up and slightly spread his arms; I could tell he was Listening for Something. The light seemed to come and go, the source of which I could not see. The breeze returned, more Strongly now, and Colder. I asked him what was happening, or what he thought was happening. He said to me:

"I may have been wrong – I See That Now. This may be more than a large-scale case of imprinting. There may be an actual Spirit Influence at work here in this house. It is...it is very subtle, almost as if it were Hiding from me. I am afraid I do not fully understand it at this moment, and that worries me a bit. Still, the story is not yet Fully Played Out; with your kind indulgence, Deputy, we should hasten to its end. There is at least one more act."

I agreed, but asked Janus if we were in an Immediate Danger. He assured me that we were most probably not, but that we should be Aware of our surroundings at all time. I in turn assured him that a Good Policeman was always so. Then, we once more returned to the archway that opened into the sitting room and watched.

The man stepped into the room. It was Dark Again, another nighttime scene. Manatee was fully-clothed but Unshaven. He glanced around a few times, as if looking for something, and began to Rummage through the room. Suddenly, the woman, the girl's mother, flew in, quite obviously In a Rage. She shouted at him:

"You bastard! What Have You Done? Where is she?"

The woman flung herself at the man and Beat Him with her fists. He simply grabbed her wrists and held her in front of him, Undisturbed and even smiling slightly. He in turn spoke to her:

"Why, Anna, I told you – Velma and I are getting Married tomorrow. I'm very sorry we can't invite you to the wedding, but it will be far, far from here, you see. Perhaps we will send you a nice letter telling you all about it. You'd like that, wouldn't you?"

The woman struggled against his Bondage, but he was too strong for her. She began to kick at him and this made the man laugh. She hurled more oaths at him:

"Sick, twisted bastard! Oh, God, why did I ever let you into this house? You have ruined us – you Have Ruined Her! She's only a Child! She is my Everything! Where did you take her? Where is she, Damn you!"

Manatee laughed again, clearly relishing the woman's Pitiful Struggle and desperation. He spoke once more to her, in a snide, condescending tone:

"Anna, my dear, dear Anna – she's gone and you'll never see here again, so don't even bother to ask. That sweet little girl is Now Mine, lock, stock and barrel. You don't have any Money, see? That's why I had to take her, to make up for your poor State of Affairs. I guess we ought to have Just Killed You – she wanted to, you know. But, now, I have a bit of time and Velma would wait an Eternity for my return, so let's see if the mother tastes as sweet as the daughter, eh?"

He released her wrists and, catching the woman Around the Waist with one hand, began to pull at her skirts with the other hand. His mouth went to her neck and he began to make Sounds of Pleasure.

The woman cried out, Shocked, and struggled against him as his hand disappeared beneath her skirts. Then, suddenly, we saw a flash and before we Scarcely Knew what was happening, a large pair of shears appeared in the woman's hand and she drove them Very Deeply into the man's neck. He screamed and blood fountained into the air. Releasing the woman, Manatee Grasped Feebly at the shears sticking out of his neck, but within seconds he dropped to the floor, Quite Dead.

Janus and I then watched as the woman began to sob; Quietly at first and then Loudly and Pitifully. She looked Wildly about the room, as if to spot her daughter, and then she paused. A look of Reflection came into her eyes then, and she wiped away her tears with a shaking hand. Looking down once at the body of Manatee, the woman stepped over it and to a small trunk at one side of the room, and From Within took out a short length of rope or cord. I could see her Set Her Jaw and pull herself up Straight and Proud. Then, she stepped through us and out of the room.

At The Moment, I heard Janus say very quietly to himself:
"We are all, every one of us, Defeated at moments like this…"
Then, in the bedroom in which we stood, the light Disappeared all-together. Janus Cautioned me to be prepared for anything. I took out my billy club and looked around the room. I could see Many Shadows, some of which did not seem to be cast by the objects in the room, but I Cannot be Sure. The breeze returned, colder than Ever Before, and it blew straight at us. There also seemed to be a Howling Sound of a kind that came along with it.
Janus shouted over the gale to me:
"McPeek, I feel as if I have Wronged you – as we stood watching those scenes, forces have Apparently Gathered in this room and Marshaled Themselves into a Direct Manifestation. I did not see it, or fully see it, and now we are Presented With a Problem. This house cannot Continue to Stand as it does now!"
I asked him what Exactly He Meant, but he did not answer. Janus stepped again into the center of the bedroom and raised his arms above his head, as if her were a Conductor at a Concert. This is

the Only Way I can think to describe it. Then, the Entire Structure began to creak and groan. I could feel a Vibration run through the house, beginning from Below and Moving Upwards to the attic.

I asked the sergeant if the Manifestation, as he called it, seemed to be one of the people we had Viewed In the Room. He shook his head, Letting Me Know that he himself did not know. I could see then that he was Concentrating and then realized that it was Janus himself that was Most Likely Shaking the house. I am not Wholly Sure what led me to that deduction but I felt Very Certain of it at that moment. I called out to him again, and Informed him that there were laws concerning Demolition and that as a Duly-Deputized Officer of the Law I could Not Allow him to demolish the house. Janus ignored me.

Let this record state that What I Did Next I did with Supreme Confidence and with all Good Intention to protect not only Sgt. Janus' well-being but that of my own. Stepping forward, I Subdued the man with my billy club and picking him up Bodily moved to exit the attic and then the house.

Janus did not stir as I carried him from the house, but all around us the structure seemed to Rebel against my actions. It was the sculpted velvet In Particular that I felt was Most Agitated and swatches of it looked to be Flying Up and At Us as I moved towards the kitchen and the back door. Once we were out and across the rear lawn, I Did Not Stop but moved us to what I deemed a Safe Distance from the structure. Then, I set Janus down and turned to Look Back at the house.

I watched as First the Roof and then the Walls Crumbled and then Fell In on Themselves. Then, the entire house collapsed with a Mighty Roar and fell with a Crash into a heap of twisted and cracked wood and shattered brick. The Cloud of Dust and Debris that arose from the event was Staggering in Size and it seemed to spread over the Entire Neighborhood.

I Became Aware then of Sgt. Janus standing by my side, now conscious and watching. I was about to turn to him and offer My

Explanation for my actions when he clamped a Firm Hand on my shoulder and said to me:

"No, no; I understand completely, Officer. You did your Duty and I would expect Nothing Less from you. In the end, my own purposes Were Served and everything is now As It Should Be. These spirits are finally laid to rest."

Later, after the firemen arrived to Make Sure there was no chance for fire at the scene, I talked with my Captain while we stood and viewed what was Left of the house. I saw Sgt. Janus turn from a last look at the Destruction and make his way back to his automobile. I Noted that he was now fully using his cane.

After Further Investigation, I have been unable to Determine what became of Miss Velma Random.

This Ends my Report of the events of April 1 and 2. I would be happy to answer any Other Questions about these events if they should arise.

"If I and the others in my profession are doing our jobs well, the average man on the street should find that he is inundated by spirit material to a lesser and lesser degree as time marches on.

"For myself, it will vary. I may have several cases in a year's time, perhaps anywhere from six to a dozen, but the next year may only encounter the supernatural twice or even three times at the most. Interestingly, I don't believe there has ever been a study that has explored the rate of ghostly occurrences in relation to times of the year - food for thought for an enterprising young psychical student.

"Let us also be clear as to the exact nature of ectoplasm. In Shudboldt's 'Musings on the Threads of Planar Construction,' he describes ectoplasm as the "blood of the beyond." In other words, he saw the substance as necessary for spiritual "well-being," the fluid, if you will, that makes their "life" possible. I do not disagree, but I have long believed that the definition needs to be expanded to not only include a blood component, but also a skin, muscle and organ comparison. That is to say that ectoplasm, to my mind, is the foundation block of spiritual existence, not just that which allows for its locomotion and "health," but the actual timber from which it is constructed."

Excerpted from "Janus Speaks!"
The Mount Airy Eagle
April 10 Edition

Chapter VII
WHEN THE RAIN COMES

You do not know me; we have never met. I do know of you, though, and I have taken the chance that you may find my story interesting. For myself, it is a complete mystery and today it seems as if it all had happened to someone else. Perhaps you can make sense of it, and I pray that you will, as it stands as the longest and most terrifying week of my life and I would like to try and understand why.

My name is Dorothy St. John and I live just outside the little village of Hope's Puddle, almost thirty miles west of your Mount Airy. I was married just last year and my husband and I came out from the city to live here in a small farmhouse that we had come to love. That was before the big rain that began two weeks ago, on April the 14th; now, I am not sure how I feel about it.

Richard, my husband, travels for his firm as a salesman and is away at least two or more weeks out of every month. Having been born into a large family with many siblings, I was not used to being so totally alone, but I steeled myself for the life we were to live and found ways to keep my hands and my mind busy while Richard was away on his trips. He himself grew up on a farm, and yearned to return to that life; I am city-educated and love to read and even dabble in writing and other creative pursuits, so perhaps you will think it strange that I chose the life of a housewife. Let me make it clear that our farmhouse was a cheerful place when we first bought it and moved in, but now...I doubt if I can ever look at it the same again.

My husband left on a Monday morning, early, before I was even out of bed myself, but we had said our goodbyes the night before.

When I awoke, the sky was clear and cloudless, bringing with it the promise of a grand and glorious day. As the hours progressed, I could see the storm rolling in and knew that by nightfall we would be in the thick of it. Who had any idea then that it would last as long as it did?

Once the sun had set, a few drops began to fall. I had brought in all my washing from the line and made sure to shut the barn up tight; we don't have any animals yet, you see, so I didn't have to contend with that at least. I could just hear the first rumblings of thunder off in the distance right after I'd finished my supper, and while I was drying the dishes I spied a few splashes of lightning.

It was when I went upstairs to prepare for bed that I looked out my window to see a lone figure standing far out in the fields, looking towards the house.

We have only neighbors on two sides of our property and neither are the kind to visit unannounced, let alone after dark. Peering through the window, which had become streaked with rain, I could make out little detail save that it appeared to be a man. I blinked, trying to discern who it might be, but the solitary figure seemed to blur and smudge in the rain and disappear. Then, it would return within a moment, pale and unmoving, standing out in the field as if lit by its own soft, internal glow. Growing more frustrated with my inability to make it out clearly, I finally threw up the window to view the figure without being hampered by the rain-streaked glass, but the very moment I did so the image of the man sank away as if it had never been there. It was after many long moments of hanging my head out the window that I came to my senses and realized I was now dampened by the rain, which had begun to fall steadily by that time.

I closed the window, wondering if I had seen the figure at all, and feeling vaguely uneasy about the entire incident I found a towel to dry my hair and re-set it for slumber. With one more glance towards the seemingly-empty fields, I climbed into bed and settled myself. I listened to the rain for a little while, now beating on the roof with a steady rhythm, and I began to feel dozy and warm. Then, with no real sense of how much time might have passed, I became aware of the fact that I had not fallen asleep, but was still lying there staring at the window. It was the same window through which I had seen the figure in the fields.

It was silent in my bedroom then, oh so deathly silent. While still lying in bed, I stared at the window, transfixed. A hand appeared on the sill from below. It was pale and thin. Then another came into view. I could not look away; I was frozen. In my mind, I knew, oh how I *knew*, what was to come next. Slowly, terribly slowly and with great purpose, a sickly-pale head then rose from below and between the two hands which gripped the sill. Oh, I could not look away!

In my mind's eye, I sketched out an image of the face that would adorn that head. I prayed it would not be as terrible as I had imagined. Then, the face did finally rise above the sill – oh! It was more than terrible! Distorted as if had long been soaking in fetid water, the face was a wicked, grinning vision with piercing eyes and toothy smile. Its lips and eyebrows curved into a leering countenance as the face looked in at me. It saw me as clearly as I saw it, and still I could not look away.

From deep inside I drew upon whatever reserves of strength I might possess to aid me at the moment. I imagined what would come next, the opening of the window, and prayed that once again my imagination would not become reality. Inch by inch, I dragged my hands up to the edge of my blanket and with a surge of energy I pulled it up and over my face, as a frightened child might to ward off the evil that they know lurks in their darkened bedrooms. The child believes the blanket will act as a shield of sorts, to protect them from the monsters that seek them out; under my blanket, I trusted in the same fashion, listening and waiting for what was to come.

Then, it was morning, and it was still raining.

Of course you will think that I had fallen asleep and dreamed the entire encounter, as I would have if someone had described it to me. I swear to you that I had not drifted off and that I did not dream that face at my window. Yes, there were no marks on the windowsill that I could see, marks that would show that someone was pulling themselves up to my window, but I ask you…would a ghost leave marks?

While making breakfast that next morning, I decided to put the event behind me. Unfortunately, it was only a preamble to what more the rain would bring.

As I cleaned the breakfast dishes and looked towards my daily routine, a word began to form in my mind. At that moment, though, I could not say what the word was for it had not yet fully formed – it remained elusive, not unlike a memory that plays around on the fringes of your memory but remains just out of sight. Whatever the word was, I could not bring it past the tip of my tongue. This was quite a bother, but I forged ahead with my day by singing out loud as many songs as I could remember in the hopes of drowning out my own thoughts.

The rain continued to fall, beating a steady rhythm on the roof. I admit that it was at first somewhat pleasant to me as I went about my tasks, helping to lift my spirits, but by the afternoon the sight of the downpour and the misty grey it had brought to the outside world served to depress me. A vague melancholy settled in and I could not divine its source, save for the rain itself, so I continued to busy myself with chores. Finally, after long hours of avoiding it, I made up my mind to check our basement for flooding.

The house itself is sound. The previous owner was steadfastly religious in keeping the structure maintained, but we were warned that if we encountered heavy rains the cellar would flood more often than not. It is a stone chamber, not an earthen one, but nevertheless it tends to collect pools of water when the rain comes. There is naught to do for it, supposedly, and I grew to hate the smell of it when it flooded; it seemed to me that the outside made its way inside and threatened the sanctity of cleanliness in our home.

I opened the door to the cellar and peered down the steps, illuminating the darkness with a candle. Seeing nothing terribly amiss, I descended into the abyss. When I reached the basement, I saw immediately that there was a smallish pool of black water off to one side – the constant rain had found its way in. Like I said, there was nothing I could do about it so I looked around for anything I needed to remove from the floor and save from the deluge. Then, while I was concentrating on that, I heard a slight squeaking noise and, holding my candle aloft, looked over at the small metal door to the coal bin. It had swung open.

Fear washed over me; why exactly I did not know at that moment. Then, a man stepped out from the darkness within the bin.

It was a wispy form, a figure more of fog than of substance, but its one hand rested on the door to the bin and had obviously opened it. The figure had no face, thank the good Lord, for if it had I would surely have fallen on the spot. As it was, I was as frozen in place as the night before in my bed. I stared, frightened. The man – if that is what it truly was – simply stood there, but I could sense malevolence in it as my heart pounded furiously in my breast and in my head.

What could it be? I wondered, but the thought died in my brain as the cloudy figure then began to move slowly towards me. A tiny part of me recognized the fact that I could see the coal bin and its door through the man. Suddenly, there came another figure. It did not come from above or from below, but seemed to float in from one side, flat and transparent, almost as if it were a photographic slide projected into the cellar and onto the misty form that advanced towards me. The new figure was dull and, again like a photographic image, out of focus; I felt as if I could see the vague outline of a person in it. When that strange phenomenon was overlaid on the menacing figure from the coal bin, that one retreated. As queerly as it had shown itself, the misty spirit dissipated and vanished entirely.

Then, my candle sputtered and extinguished itself. I was plunged into total darkness. Finally and blessedly freed from my stupor, my legs drove me towards the stairs and finding them I scrabbled upwards, clawing my way to the top and through the door. One again in the light, I breathlessly threw closed the cellar door and latched it securely. Skirts torn and bloodied on palms and knees from my panicked flight from the basement, I fled to my bedroom and locked myself in tight. The rain continued to fall, uncaring.

I stayed in my room for the rest of that day and into the night, forgoing dinner and the rest of my tasks. Sitting on my bed, I rocked back and forth, listening to the rain and praying that Richard would come home early from his trip. Maybe, I thought, the rain would have washed out a bridge somewhere and, his train unable to continue, he would turn around and return to me. I wept like a child, berating myself for such a senseless hope; I would be alone in the house for several more days.

Yes, I contemplated leaving and trying to make my way to one of the neighbors, but every time I looked out the window the rain seemed to come down even harder and I could see nothing but great pools of water and long tracts of mud barring my way. No, I would have to stay and be subjected to whatever was happening in the house.

When the nagging thoughts of the word I could not remember returned to vex me, I went looking for a medicinal powder that Richard had once fetched from the doctor for me, one that was to ease my mind "in times of great adversity." I found it and mixing it with some water drank it down greedily. It did serve to relax me somewhat and I managed to undress and crawl into bed. Lying there, I again listened to the rain and the thunder and eventually fell into a dreamless sleep.

The next morning, Wednesday, I awoke to the rain. It registered on my thoughts as a common occurrence, so used to its sound was I by that time. Oh, in the back of my mind I wished it would stop, questioned its strength and stamina, but a lethargy had come over me by the third day that clouded my consciousness. I got up from my bed and went to a chair and sat; it was time to have a talk with myself.

I asked myself if I truly believed the things I had seen since the rain began, and whether or not the storm brought them in. I did not know. I still do not know to this day. I hoped I was not going mad; I had heard of people going mad in times of isolation, but I looked deep into myself and decided I was still sane...but still I could not explain the ghostly images that appeared to be seeking me out. Again, I am hoping you can decipher this mystery.

I began to feel very, very hungry, not having eaten for almost twenty-four hours, and almost as soon as I thought of food there came a loud crashing sound from downstairs. I stood up dully and went to go see what it was.

Nothing looked amiss from my vantage point at the top of the stairs, so I proceeded to descend and approach the kitchen – and the door to the cellar. I could hear thunder off in the distance as I entered my kitchen and saw that a wall rack that was mounted near the basement door had fallen…no, that is not right. It looked like it had been wrenched from the wall to which it was bolted or, perhaps, pushed out from behind. I stood a long time and stared at the door to the cellar and finally made up my mind to open it and see how much flooding had occurred below. With leaden arms and hands I unlatched the door and slowly opened it.

I was greeted with a fetid, brackish odor, strong and swampy. Below, I could hear a dripping sound; somehow, I knew that the basement was truly flooded then. Taking up a candle, I lit it and, steeling myself, prepared to go down the stairs. Almost as soon as my foot hovered over the first step, a foul breeze blew out my candle. Then, from somewhere in the inky blackness at the bottom of the stairs, from a dark, dark place that could not exist in my own basement, came a voice.

Writing this now, I can scarcely describe it in any accurate fashion. Neither male nor female, it was both deep and hollow and seemed to create its own echo. I wonder now if it truly spoke out loud there in my house, or if I heard it solely inside my mind. The voice spoke but a single word, and that word was like a searing brand in the air:

STENNDEC

It was the word that I could not bring to my mind earlier.

I slammed the door shut and turn to flee the kitchen – I am not sure if I even latched the door. The word rang in my head, chilling me to my very soul, as I ran from the room with every intention of retreating to my bedroom. I rounded the corner from the dining room to the hallway and saw that something was coming down the stairs.

It was misty and vaguely man-shaped, like the thing in the basement, but not as defined. It glowed from within with a feeble light, like a candle seen through water. I screamed. It continued on its way down, step by step, floating with stately malevolence. I backed up against the wall; with the kitchen behind and this horrible thing in front of me, I had nowhere to go. Oh, God! The thought of it even now terrifies me.

Then, once again, there came the strange, flattened image of a man which superimposed itself over the thing on the stairs. This occurred just as the wispy spirit neared the bottom step. It seemed much more well-formed than before and I have a sense that it was indeed a man, or the image of one, and that he looked calm and serene. I am almost quite sure his eyes were closed.

The two images froze as they overlapped and the temperature in the room grew suddenly frigid. A stand-off seemed to take place and the shape on the stairs began to lose substance, first breaking up into patches of smoky smudges and then fading before my eyes. The image of the man disappeared, also. After many minutes the ticking of a clock came to my ears and I found myself stretched out on the floor of the hallway, sobbing. I was alive and whole and the rain continued to fall.

I shall not write the word out again. I could barely write it once. It fills me with such terror and foreboding that to even look at it is almost more than I can bear. I have studied a few languages, but it did not seem to be of a kind that I recognize…it seems something entirely unearthly. What it means or why it was spoken in my house, I cannot say, but I prayed that I might be able to forget it.

After seeing the thing on the stairs I felt sure that my house was no longer a place of safety. I admit that I went a little mad then, for I raced through the entire house searching for, well, I am not sure. Holes in the walls? Signs of ingress? And why should I have been concerned about physical points of access when these spirits made their way in seemingly at will? Again, I went a little mad, I'm afraid.

I checked every window for leaking and looked into every nook and cranny for cracks in the plaster that might allow the rain to seep in. Every spot in the house was checked save the basement; there I would not go ever again. I imagined the water was frighteningly high there and to emphasize the point as it occurred to me, a great peal of thunder rang out and the rain grew even stronger. I shook all over in horror when I heard it.

When I had finished my maniacal tear through the house, I retreated once again to my room upstairs. I took with me provisions of food, water and books, determined to lock myself in and wait out the storm. A tiny, still-rational part of my brain told me that it could not last forever.

By the time I was ready to begin my enforced incarceration in the bedroom, it was early evening. I stopped at the bathroom to splash some water in my face and to look at myself in the mirror. As I had assumed, I looked a fright. Dark circles had appeared under my eyes and my skin had grown pale and my hair completely disheveled; I looked like the madwoman I believed myself to be. You mustn't think me too vain – I am a woman after all.

Realizing how late it had become and wanting to secure myself in my room, I hurriedly turned to leave the bathroom. As I did, my foot slipped on something on the floor and I lost my balance. I remember reaching out to catch myself but slipped again and then – blackness.

I don't know how long I laid there on the floor of the bathroom, but when I awoke it was very dark. I touched my head and felt a great knot there and could also feel something sticky along the side of my face. I guessed that I had hit my head on the bathtub when I fell. Once realization of what had happened washed over me, panic soon followed; I needed to be secure in my room. Yes, the feeling of panic gripped me tightly and I stood up despite the supreme dizziness that fell upon me. I lit a candle and went to leave, but stopped when I caught sight of myself in the mirror.

There I was, dried blood along my temple and down one cheek – and someone was standing behind me.

It was Thursday! I had been knocked unconscious and now it was the next day and the fourth spirit had found me! Once again I froze, cemented in place by the ghastly apparition in the mirror of a man in what looked like military clothing and with blood streaking his own face. Oh, it was a nightmare! His eyes were glossed over and his mouth hung open and that vital spark of life utterly and completely missing from his frame – and he was drenched, completely soaked through from the rain. Because of the blood, I thought at first that perhaps I was seeing double from the blow to my head, that the spirit was but another image of myself, but I was frighteningly wrong.

I could not scream, though every nerve in my body stood on edge and urged me to do so. I remember hearing inarticulate gurgling noises and then realized it was me who was making them. Behind and over the man, I could see water dripping down from the ceiling – that must be what I had slipped on. Oh, if I had not fallen I would have made it to my room before midnight had come!

A strange jactitation came over me and my hand jerked out and the candle, still in my hand, fell from its holder and to the floor. The room was enveloped in darkness and this broke the queer spell I was under. Terrified that grimy, wet hands would reach out from the darkness, I fled from the room and slammed the bathroom door shut behind me. I ran to my bedroom and locked myself in as lightning flashed in the sky and illuminated my way, and all the while that word of horror echoed in my brain.

Once inside, I paced round and round the room, my nerves screaming at me to flee the house. My head pounded and I looked for my tincture – I had no real hope that it would soothe me, but I had little else of comfort to seek. Eventually, was able to stop pacing and sit down on my bed. Once settled, I tried to think through the events of the last few days and try to make sense of them.

I reminded myself again that it was now Thursday, and with that fourth day of Richard being gone came the fourth ghost. I was quite sure then that each day of the storm would bring another spirit to terrify me. But why? What did they seek? And, who were they…in life, that is.

Despite the horrifying circumstances, I found myself ruefully chuckling: here I was, attempting to guess at the motives of things from beyond when only days ago I was not certain that such things even existed. Certainly, I had heard stories of phantasms and hauntings, but being somewhat of a pragmatic person I found them to be merely a form of entertainment, tales to be told to liven a party or to give small children the frightened giggles. But, now, I was trapped in my own house and defending myself against…against… what? Vengeful spirits of the dead? Oh, why were they haunting me? What had I done to upset them? Or was it that I was merely in their path?

I also wondered about the image of the man who had saved me twice before; why had it not come this time to my aid? No, that was a dangerous thought. I could not rely on such a thing; I knew little of the malevolent phenomenon that was vexing me – how could I hope that there was also a benevolent form that could also help me?

As I thought on these things, I made a circuit of my bedroom and checked for leaks. When I was satisfied that there were none and that the windows and doors were secure, I allowed myself to eat a bite of apple and some bread and then crawled into bed, fully clothed. As I had done before, I listened to the rain and remembered when, long ago, it was a pleasant sound to me.

For the most part, true sleep eluded me and I rose sometime in the early morning on Friday. I looked around my bed, expecting to see more spirits come to assail me, but it was clear I was alone – for the moment, at least. I was utterly fatigued and could not see how I would make it through to the end of the rainstorm, whenever that might be.

In an effort to make myself feel a little better, I changed my clothes and went in search of a book. After a long perusal of the volumes at hand, I finally picked an innocuous tome on, of all things, butterflies and settled in to read. It was not long before the steady drumming of the rain on the roof derailed my reading and I began to think about the image of the man who had come to my aid on two separate occasions. Who might it have been? I pondered. He appeared, well, serene and composed, as if he were sleeping, but the more I dwelled on his face it occurred to me that it was something more than that.

Could it have been an image of our Lord? The man in the image did not necessarily look like the traditional illustrations of the Savior, but I am also not so close-minded to believe that He absolutely appeared on Earth as a bearded man with long, flowing locks. The strange picture of the man that came to me was clean-shaven and with short, somewhat tousled hair. I mean, surely he might have been…oh, I suppose that I was of little faith to not be certain at the time.

Then, like a bolt of lightning, it occurred to me that the man, with his serene countenance and pale skin might have been deceased.

A weird, crawling sensation came over me and the sound of dripping came to my ears before I could ponder that thought further. I looked up with dread to see a drop of water fall from within the fireplace onto the logs below. The chimney – why hadn't I thought of that before?

I bolted out of my chair, sending my book flying across the room, and dove for the flue lever; I grabbed it and twisted it, shutting the flue up tight. Frightened beyond measure, I tried to soak up the rain that had made it in with my skirts and then stumbled around to try and make a fire in the heath. Finally, after much effort, I had a small blaze going, but it soon began to smoke and I, with great reluctance, reopened the flue. Let the rain attempt an assault through a blazing fire, I thought, while I kept watch on it through the night.

The reality of that honorable notion did not exactly match my intent. I had settled into my chair again to keep watch over the fire and stoked it and fed it when it seemed to diminish; on occasion I could heard a slight hissing sound from drips of water that fell into the blaze. I was sure I could keep it going through the night and perhaps find some dry wood in the morning…

With supreme effort I fought to keep my eyes open, but the sound of the rain combined with the cheerful crackling of the fire to sing a lullaby of sleep. At some indeterminate hour I realized I had dozed and, looking over at the fireplace, witnessed the price of my folly. A tendril of wispy smoke, whiter than it should have been, wound its way from the open flue and under the upper edge of the fireplace opening. It seemed to have a mind of its own, testing the height of the flames and my powers as a sentry. Then, I watched as the head of the cloudy tendril split and before my very eyes formed into what I can only call fingers – it became nothing less than a pale imitation of a human hand, curving like the head of a cobra. I held my breath; perhaps it could not actually see me, if it indeed was able to see anything in the proper sense. Ah, the tension that wove itself through the air of that room! I did not feel as frozen as I had when confronted by the previous spirits, but nonetheless I remained motionless lest this unwanted visitor determine my exact position in the room.

Not knowing what I should do – or could do – I watched as the flames grew shorter and the spectral hand grow bolder. Its finder seemed to grip the edge of the opening as if it would pull an entire body down through the flue and into the room – if that were to have happened, I would surely have died on the spot. If only I could have dared to move and feed the fire! Alas, I sat curled in my chair, feebly protected by blankets and awaiting…what, I was not sure.

Then, the flames licked a little higher and suddenly they shot up with furious force. The ghostly appendage shrank back immediately, as if afraid of the blaze. To my astonishment a face appeared in the fire! It was the face of the clean-shaven man once again, oh Lord bless him, whoever he was! His image resided completely in the tongues of flame, a serene as before, and in direct juxtaposition to the fury of the fire. The ghostly hand swatted at the blaze, but, perhaps in resignation, it formed back into a more solid tendril and pulled itself back up the flue. In a moment, it was gone and the image of the man dissipated with the once-more dying flames.

You may believe that I was comforted to be saved once again, but in truth I was even more discomfited; this was the fifth ghastly phantom to approach me and I was certain that more would come. In fact, as I sat there and watched the fire I knew for a certainty that a sixth would come, and then a seventh and with the seventh would come death...my own.

At some point, at some undetermined hour, I stood at my bedroom window and watched as my barn collapsed into a heap of rotted wooden timbers.

By that time I was almost completely numb and perhaps more than a little mad. I had risen from my chair, not having slept a wink after the incident with the fireplace, at what I thought were voices outside in the yard. I thought that they might be those of someone come to rescue me, or perhaps even Richard returned from his trip, but I was not to be that fortunate. Having pulled back the curtains and looking down upon the ground outside my house, I saw no rescuers, only my entire barn crumble and fall in on itself.

Let them have the barn, I thought. Let them have the basement. Let them have the whole wide world to rain upon; they shall not have me. But, as soon as I had made my declaration, depression and lethargy once again overtook me and I surrendered to the pounding of the rain. Friday came and went and I could not tell you now what I did for the entire day inside my room.

I rose on Saturday to great peals of thunder and sharp stabs of lightning; it seemed that the storm had grown angrier. I had decided that the demolition of the barn was a kind of retribution for the defeat of the fireplace – they had made their sally and were repelled. Our barn was all they could muster as a form of revenge.

On the outside, I was sure I appeared quite a fright, as I had made sure to cover the one small mirror I kept in the bedroom and so had no way to check myself. No matter, I thought, for once the sixth spirit made its presence known, my path was set. The day before, I had burned my last shred of defiance; on Saturday I was once again resigned to my fate. The seventh apparition would most likely be the most terrifying of all, as the number seven played in and out of so many of the world's mythologies and systems of belief – seven was significant, and not always so lucky.

At some time in the afternoon – it might even have been early evening – a sound came to my ears, at first low and elusive and then growing in prominence. One part of me recognized it finally as a bugle. I stood and moved like an automaton to the window, then pulled back the curtains to look out into the yard. At first I saw nothing, only hearing the melancholy, otherworldly tune, but then I saw a mist rising up above the ruins of the barn. It was like a sheet of sand, in a way, falling upwards and coalescing in the air, forming a more distinct figure – the sixth spirit.

This shade appeared as cloudy as the others – incredible that it could hold any shape at all in the rain – and finally took on the trappings of a man with a small horn. I was sure that it was intended to be a soldier, a bugler blowing a dirge. Its tune wafted about, threading in and out of my consciousness, but with some last parcel of rebellion within me I resisted the overwhelming urge to open the window and allow the tune full entry. I also tried to dispel the nagging notion that it was to be a death knell.

I let the curtain fall back into place and returned to my chair. Eventually, the sad sounds died away and I sat silently weeping; not for myself, but for Richard. Oh, I grew more depressed at the thought of how he would find me if he ever returned.

Sunday arrived and with it more rain. To write of it now brings back the feelings of leaden melancholy that possessed me on that day. I did not even bother to rise from where I had been curled up in my chair when day came – it looked to be the same as the six days that had come and gone previously. The only difference to Sunday was that I dully wondered how the end would come and the irony that it would be on the Lord's Day.

With not a little effort, I tried to eat and drink some water, but I realized I was horrified at the thought of allowing the life-giving liquid into my body. My hand shook uncontrollably as I held the glass in front of me and I let it slip from my grip and shatter on the floor. I sat for long minutes then and composed myself, organizing my thoughts and in effect my life. Poor Richard, I thought; coming home to his dear wife to find…to find…ah, I cannot even write the words now, some time later.

Finally, I rose from my seat and turned to the windows. There, I drew back the curtains and began my lonely vigil.

Outside, the rain still fell and our yard was almost completely covered in pools of dark water. The deluge fell in sheets that wandered up and down our property, soaking everything in their wake. The timbers of the ruined barn sat like the broken hull of a once-mighty ship, dashed onto the rocks and all hands lost. I took in this sorry scene, but it made little difference to me in the state that I was in. My focus was on the fields that stretched out and way from the house.

Far off in the distance the rain had obscured the horizon and blurred the trees that dotted the landscape; it was all-together a smoky plateau, drenched in moisture from the days-long deluge. I stared at it for quite a long time before I began to make out shapes in that mist, many forms that seemed to bob up and down in unison far off in the fields. Soon, I discerned what looked like heads and then what appeared to be shafts of some sort slung over what I imagined might be the shoulders that supported the heads.

It was, I thought at that moment, a regiment of soldiers with shouldered rifles marching towards our homestead.

At once separate and at the same time part of the mist that surrounded them, the ghostly heads and shoulders moved as a unit, slowly and surely, in my direction. The sight of it made me catch my breath and then outraged me – what was I to do? Oh, it was a terrible, terrible sight to behold; a marching band of spirits on target for my home, perhaps whipped up in determination after their scouts had made some inroads on the enemy…me. Why they would be here and how they were connected with the constant downfall of rain those past several days I could not fathom, but suffice to say, my feeling of despair grew to monumental proportions at the sight.

I looked all around, through my room and across the yard and over the ruined barn and then out into the field but there was nothing I could see of hope or charity. But, somehow, a small flame began to grow inside me, first born of panic, then anger and then a kind of fury at being the victim of these spirits. My face grew hot as I viewed the bobbing heads of the spirit regiment and remembered every injustice their advance shades had laid on my head in my own house. Feeling that fire, I stoked it and stoked it until I allowed it to grow red-hot and threaten to smolder the curtains and windowsill before me. One haunting a day was enough to cow me, but the sight of the evil that marched my way was too much for me to bear.

Grasping the latch of the window, I paused, gathered my strength and then flung open the window. Cold, stinging rain slapped at me instantly, but I gritted my teeth and pressed my face through it and outside. The drops, big and wet, served to steel me and they hissed into nothingness from my inner flame.

I screamed. I let loose with all my fury, all my pent-up emotions of frustration and shame and impotency, and spewed them across the fields and at my attackers. I cursed, I vowed, I swore with all my being that they, whoever the might be, would not have my house of myself for their revenge or even their amusement. I could scarcely believe the words that I spat at them, so vehement were they. Oh God, please forgive me...I had nothing else with which to fight them...

The regiment paused. As the last oath left my mouth I saw that the heads seemed to stop and prick up at my screams. I fancied I could see their egg-white eyes scanning the house and narrowing in confusion; perhaps I had given them what no other of their victims had before. The rain fell even harder and thunder and lightning whipped up suddenly overhead.

The spectral soldiers stood their ground for a minute, then two and then three. Then, they renewed their forward advancement.

I was spent. I knew of nothing else in me to hurl at them. I sagged against the window frame and prepared for the worst, but knowing I had given it my all. If I were to be conquered by this invading force, it would be as a whole person and not the shell I had become over the past few days.

Came a light. A bright light, not such as the lightning, but purer, if that can be believed – perhaps you know of which I speak. The light came in from the side and swept towards the fields like a sheet of bright, white paper hovering above the tall grass and cutting its way towards the advancing soldiers. It glided soundlessly like a phantom itself and cut directly in front of the regiment; the first line of the heads dropped down into the mist that surrounded them and suddenly I saw their ghostly rifles peep out as if the men had dropped to one knee and prepared to fire.

The bright sheet of phantom quality blazed like the sun and sliced through the ranks of the ghostly infantry like a knife through butter. All-white flames rose from its surface and at that moment I saw the image of my savior, the serene man, appear their. Several yards across, the sheet of fire dove towards the rest of the soldiers and into their ranks. The heads bobbed and toppled and I thought I could hear the echoes of spectral screams as they fell.

I found myself once again leaning out my window and hurling my own screams to drown out those of the soldiers. As I yelled, the fires of the phantom image stood taller and brighter, or so it seemed, and I fancied I was lending my energies to its sortie. The fields blazed with light and mist and the sounds of rifle shots and the screams of men dying for a second time.

I knew not when it ended. It seemed to go on forever.

My husband found me lying in a pool of rain water in the yard with a piece of splintered wood from the barn in my hands. He was, of course, quite concerned for me. I assured him that the trouble was over and that I would be up and on my feet to properly welcome him home, but only after several days of sleep.

Sometime later, I awoke in my bed with Richard and the doctor hovering over me, grave looks on their faces. I told them I was feeling much better and then waited for the physician to leave before explaining myself to my husband.

146

Richard believes my tale, or at least he tells me he does. He told me he would never, ever leave my side again, but I told him that was him being foolish…I would go with him on his trips from here on out. We will be a team.

So many questions I have about my travails and little in the way of answers. But, there is one question I did have answered and that is why I write this record and send it to you, sir. You see, I believe I know the identity of my savior.

Richard had gathered up all the newspapers that had sat waiting for me at our little post office box in town, and had given them to me to read while I convalesced. They were a little bit out of date by a week or two, but it was pleasant to look through them and forget my ordeal while I did so.

One news article caught my attention, a notice of an adventure of one Sgt. Janus, of Mount Airy.

In the story, the sergeant had aided a Mount Airy police officer in an investigation of a derelict house that had been, as the story said, "the sad repository for escaped criminals and a hoax of major proportions." A picture accompanied the article, showing the police officer and Sgt. Janus.

I recognized that man as my supernatural rescuer: *you*, sir.

If I may ask; what does it all mean? Why did your image appear to be that of dead man? What was that word which I heard issue forth from my cellar? It haunts me still, you see. I am sure we have never met before, sir, for I would remember such a unique person as yourself and your profession, but my head whirls with questions over the entire affair – can you offer me any explanations? Did you come to my aid, or am I the victim of an unhealthy and overactive imagination brought about by too much solitude?

I have heard that you like to collect records of your cases from your clients; I cannot claim to be such but, please, if you can, write back to me at the address on my envelope and help me in my quest for answers. I would greatly appreciate it, sir. I will not say it is driving me insane, for perhaps that is a destination at which I have already arrived.

As to the rain, it did stop, of course, though the papers say it only fell for a few days, not seven. Our basement still has water in it, but Richard could find no signs of leaks in the ceilings of the house. I would like to protest, but I will not; I know what I know.

Strange, how connected we are all to water, body and soul; the source of life itself is, for some, a source of pleasure and fascination, yet for others a source of great fear. My mind is not yet made up in which camp I will ultimately pitch my tent.

"Firstly, I must state that beyond honesty, politeness is always the best policy when dealing with the para-natural. Too often, I run up against those who feel within them the desire to communicate with spirits themselves – and I must be honest with them when they ask for my advice in doing so. I must warn them that approaching the subject on their own may open one up to all manner of troubles if one is not prepared for such untoward contact. Before diving into a situation where a spirit could potentially be hostile, I would always err on the side of caution and call in a professional first. Granted, yes, you may have met up with a poor soul who wants only the singular solace of human company, but you may also just as easily encountered a vengeful shade whose only goal is to vex the living and extract as much revenge on them as possible from beyond the grave.

"By taking this all into consideration, I believe you will see that the choice is an easy one: do not go it alone."

Excerpted from "Janus Speaks!"
The Mount Airy Eagle
April 10 Edition

Chapter VIII
THE UNFINISHED RECORD

"Can a ghost kill?"

It is, I believe, a valid and straightforward question, and one that I, after extensive research, have learned has never truly been answered. My name is C. Aldrin Blaylock and I intend to remedy that.

There are numerous accounts through the centuries of man's encounters with the spirit realm and of deaths that seem to be related to or stem from such encounters, but I hereby put forth the conjecture that it has never been proven as an absolute that a ghost, that is, the body-less spirit or soul of human being, is able to directly and with intent bring about the demise of a living person. Surely, there have been documented cases of deaths involving the general influence of spirits, the so-called "frightened to death" rationale, yet I find those of spurious pedigree and as such they do not have a place in my conjecture. I believe a ghost, once thought to be an intangible entity, has the innate ability to make direct, sustained physical contact and, in doing so, possess the ability to kill.

I begin this account poised on the first step of a journey that should not only prove this theory of mine, but, in turn, enforce and solidify my standing in the larger para-psychical community. Once I have conducted my experiments in the field, I fully intend to use these very notes to write a much more in-depth paper on the subject and submit it for publication in one of the several respected journals of our profession. I do this as a service to my fellow para-psychiatrists, so that together we may expand our knowledge and bring our vocation fully into the new century as a fact-based science, worthy to stand with the other sciences as an equal and a peer.

For the record, I have attended both Oxford and Harvard, with my doctorate studies in paranormal reasoning and meta-reality discourse through Miskatonic. Currently, I sit as a junior member on the board of directors for Walpurgis & Tetch, as well as holding the position of Assistant Editor on the *Humphries Supernatural Record*. Just last year, I was awarded the Scott Medal of Achievement in Extranormal Research, a proud moment in my career, and I have over sixty hours of experience in the field.

Herewith, I register the date and time of my first official record entry for this case:

APRIL 26, 10:32 AM

The case in question has been referred to by several appellations, but I prefer that of Holdfeldt in his *Spirits for Spelunkers*: "The Ghost of Old Man's Cave."

It is a fascinating case, and one that I feel has been ignored by other investigators; why this would be, I cannot say. Here is a rough sketch of it: the natural cave lies some seventy miles south of the city in a densely forested area that covers the foothills of a nearby mountain chain; it is a remote spot and accessible only on foot after a two-day hike from the nearest road. The cave itself was reputedly discovered in 1697 by an itinerant preacher and his two young sons, but its standing as a supernatural wellspring did not come about until the 1820s. It was during that time that the first death in or near the cave was reported.

Here is where I find the most fascination with the case. Since then, seven deaths in all have been recorded, all of them of a similar type: the nature of each victim's demise was attributed to strangulation. Such a manner of death occurs, in most cases, when one person takes it upon themselves to rob another of life; I believe those cases normally outweigh those of accidental strangulation. Old Man's Cave is, as I stated, a remote area with no human population, a situation maintained throughout the centuries. The reported deaths all showed very clear signs of purposeful malice – the mark of fingers around crushed windpipes - and none of an accidental nature; not one of the seven or eight deaths at the cave were from someone tripping and falling into vines or other constricting foliage – they were murdered. The facts are clear. They were murdered by the Ghost of Old Man's Cave.

I propose to travel to the site, make a thorough reconnoiter of the entire area and, after regular and documented observation, determine if a) the willful spirit of a deceased person inhabits the cave, and, if so, b) that it is responsible for the murder of several human beings, and c) how such a thing is possible.

For these purposes, I will also seek the involvement in my expedition of the foremost living authority on spirits and the supernatural, Sgt. Janus of Mount Airy.

Sgt. Roman Janus is something of an idol of mine, a towering figure in the profession who has made great strides in both the occult sciences and in supernatural defense, though, I must say, I feel that the scope of his research and studies has begun to stagnate and atrophy. I mean no disrespect to the man; as I said, he has done much as a trailblazer after centuries of superstitious leanings among investigators, but one must eventually bow to the march of science and recalibrate one's thinking to allow for new theories and practices. Sgt. Janus is still an active figure, yes, and we still owe him a great debt for his work, but I fear that he is in danger of becoming a living example of an extinct breed.

Regardless, to secure his services for an investigation into the Old Man's Cave situation would be a coup for me, both professionally and personally. I have met Janus only once, at an exhibition a few years ago when the "Spirit-Breaker" entered into a sort of competition with the Great Houdini himself, an event orchestrated by the magician to debunk Janus' abilities, but one that served to only stymie him. Meeting Sgt. Janus backstage was a tangible thrill for me, a relative neophyte at the time, but I must admit that I was somewhat embarrassed for the man to feel he had to prove the very real existence of ghosts to such an inveterate and infamous witch-hunter.

I plan to leave for the sergeant's home just outside of Mount Airy in a few hours, and present him with my plans for the expedition. I am sure that in the face of such well-rounded reasoning and the desire to further our knowledge of the all-too-scarce information on murderous spirits, Sgt. Janus will happily join me on my journey.

APRIL 26, 3:04 PM

Sgt. Janus has refused my invitation. As I sit here in my automobile outside his house and record my thoughts, I must state for the record that I cannot fathom the man or his reasons.

Admittedly, I arrived at Janus House unannounced, but felt certain that upon showing my credentials that I would be received. I was greeted at the door by a woman who did not introduce herself, but who I guessed to be Janus' housekeeper. She had an odd quality to her and seemed almost emotionless until, when I had politely insisted to see the man of the house, she arched one eyebrow slightly and agreed to take him my card. When she returned, I was told that Janus would see me.

"But you must not tax him too much," she added with a piercing gaze. "He is resting."

I was led through the house – a most amazing and exceedingly labyrinthine place – and to a room the woman referred to as the Vivarium. Once through its door, I found myself in what can only be described as a small forest inside a gigantic glass room. The woman had disappeared before I could ask if I was in the right place, so I began to stroll around. While I did so, I experienced the most curious feeling of being watched from all sides, as if I was in a terrarium or some such. Most disconcerting.

Then, I stumbled upon Sgt. Janus himself. He was seated in a clearing, sort of sprawled out on a lounge chair, reading from a leather-bound book and resting his head in one hand. He looked tired. When he saw me, he smiled, marked his place and, setting the volume down on a small table at his side, rose and greeted me. I spied the title of the book, one with which I was, unfortunately, not familiar: *High Etheric Displacement in Reconstructive Algorithms.*

"Ah, Blaylock," he said, extending his hand. "It is good to see you again. How may I be of assistance?"

Roman Janus is of what I would call indeterminate age, but I would guess that he is no more than fifty years old. Of average height and build and dressed in the clothes of a soldier, he struck me as a man from a previous, bygone era. Eccentricity seems to be prerequisite for many in our line of work, apparently.

I came right to the point and told him of my studies and my intentions for the expedition, including a somewhat broad hint that I might be interested in his co-authoring the paper I propose to write. Janus' entire demeanor grew quite serious then and he asked me to sit down. I was about to say that I did not care to take his chair, but then noticed that, inexplicably, there was another that I had not seen when I came into the clearing.

"My good sir," he said, after we were both sitting and facing each other. "Let me be very frank with you, if I may: please do not go to that site. You are ill-prepared for such an ordeal."

I was taken aback by the tone of his voice. I had expected some hesitancy or perhaps even a wish to lead the expedition himself, but not outright refusal.

"Sgt. Janus," I replied. "I do not understand you, sir. I admit I have much to assemble in the way of equipment and provisions, but I assure you that –"

"No," he interrupted. "Please forgive me for being obscure. What I mean to say is that you are unprepared in mind and spirit for such a case. Please, I imply no slight or insult by this, Blaylock, but Old Man's Cave is a site I would try and stop anyone, anyone at all, from visiting. I would not go there myself, even.

"See here; I understand that it appears, on the surface, to be a case that has much to recommend itself to a young man such as yourself, a devotee of occult research, but others have tried to peel back the veil around that area and expose its mysteries and each time they have failed and failed miserably. The spirit or spirits there are strong – do you see? Far stronger than any one of us, even the most gifted and experienced among our lot. Please, I beg of you: do not go there, if you value your life and your eternal soul. You know not with what you may tamper, my friend."

I protested, despite his solemn expression and words and recognition of his sincerity. "But, Janus, it is only a haunting, like many others. Yes, there is an element to it that seems dangerous, but it fits –"

"Listen to me," he said, grabbing my arm and holding it in steel-like grip. "I know this case. It is far older than you know or may have imagined. Some say the story comes to us from the indigenous people of this land or perhaps from even further back into pre-history. Do you truly believe it is merely the ghost of a grizzled prospector, a man who was wronged by his fellows and died with thoughts of vengeance burning through him? Blaylock, my dear Blaylock, I say to you again, and search your own thoughts for you know it to be true – you are not experienced enough to tackle this case on your own. I cannot in all good conscience allow you to mount this expedition and endanger yourself."

"Then come with me," I implored him. "If I am such a babe in the woods, such a drooling idiot, than I will bow to your own vast knowledge and experience and invite you to lead the team to the site and take the first crack at this spirit…"

Janus sat back, weary and pale. He ran a hand over his forehead and I could feel the desperation emanating from his frame.

"No," he said, quietly. "No, I have…recently decided to decrease the amount of outside cases I take on, choosing instead to increase my studies here at home and see those few clients who can come to me. I am sorry, truly."

That was that, from what I could see. The great Sgt. Janus had turned me down. I stood up, bid him a good day and turned to leave. Then, I heard him softly call my name.

"I hope you won't think of me too disparagingly, my friend," he said. "But please believe me when I say I speak from experience. Old Man's Cave is not for you, not yet."

Janus has done one thing for me, at least; he has made me all the more determined to go. I am not sure what he hoped to accomplish with his heavy-handed talk, but perhaps he is not the man I thought he was – or at least not anymore. It was sad to see how much his star has fallen and how much he's allowed himself to go to pot, but it will serve as a reminder to me to stay the course and conquer the problems I have laid out for myself.

Wait, I can see someone from the house approaching my machine...

APRIL 26, 4:06 PM

An incredible turn of events: Sgt. Janus has deigned to accompany me on my expedition to Old Man's Cave. His housekeeper came out and told me that her employer had had a change of heart and wished to talk to me again.

Janus greeted me in a sitting room off the main entrance hall and apologized for his earlier reluctance. He said he'd be happy to travel with me to the site and, in his words, "guide me on this most serious of investigations."

I must remember that this is quite a victory, both personally and for all those who delve into the unknown, but I cannot help but think that Janus only agreed because he still sees me as someone who needs to be sheltered from that same unknown. Regardless, I shall prove to him that I am my own man and a capable scientific investigator in my own right.

As F. G. Calliope said in his *What this World Is*, "As you write your own chronicle, beware of editors."

APRIL 28, 7:45 PM

The last two days have been taken up with all the planning and preparations for the expedition that I have had little time to make entries in this journal, but I now have a few minutes to spare to bring it up to date.

The preparations have included the acquisition of the entirety of the gear we will need for our two-day hike and for making camp in the great outdoors, as well as all the provisions for the crew. I have also procured a suitable camera and tripod arrangement, in the hopes that we will be able to document the expedition photographically – the camera will also be put to use should we find ourselves in a position to capture the spirit itself on film.

In regards to the para-normal aspect of the investigation, I must admit that the pertinent equipment has been something more of a challenge to organize. The great majority of modern ghost-hunting has concerned itself with that of buildings and other man-made structures, and so the necessary implements are not often the same for outdoor examinations. Still, I have chosen the very best in flash-lights and other such sundry items so as to insure we are as up-to-date as possible in our search. Holdfeldt, of course, has provided several avenues for equipment, and I have also found worthy suggestions in Beamish's *The Compleat Searcher's Bible* and in Stark's *Ghosts: A Guide for the Unafraid*.

I'm very happy to report that the entire expedition has been generously funded by the *Humphries Supernatural Record*; when I told the owners of the paper that Sgt. Janus himself had accepted an invitation to take part in the investigation, their coffers graciously opened. The editors of the *Record* are also of the hope that I may care to publish my paper through them, but that is not something I feel I must cement at this moment, as I could very likely take the work to a much more prestigious outfit for publication – I am sure they would understand.

I have not heard from Janus since I left his house the day before yesterday, but he assured me he would be joining us three days from now when the expedition departs from the city for the wilderness. I take the man at his word; although, of course, the journey would still proceed without him, I believe he knows his own name and reputation now have a stake in its success.

The crew shall consist of myself, as Lead Investigator; Sgt. Janus, assisting; Jackson Morrow, a guide I have hired who is familiar with the area around the cave; a bearer who goes by the unlikely moniker of Tiny Weymouth, and a driver hired by Morrow who will stay behind at the base camp we will establish before the two-day overland walk.

For myself, one of the more exciting additions to our crew comes in the form of an animal; a canine, to be precise. Morrow suggested to me that we bring along his dog, and once I pondered the possibilities I realized what an opportunity such a team member would present. Our four-footed friends are known to have a unique affinity for the supernatural of a kind not truly found in humans. Morrow's dog may also afford me another new wrinkle to my study of this case and should make for an intriguing footnote in my eventual paper.

We leave, as I have stated, three days from now, and I feel very optimistic for the entire endeavor. I should like to say that Janus' inclusion has made all the difference, but I shall resist that urge and trust to sound scientific principles to tip the scales in our favor on this journey.

MAY 1, 11:36 PM

I feel a cloud of negativity settling in over our little band. As I sit here in my tent, looking out over the base camp we have erected just off the road and, writing down my thoughts, I am determined to throw off this feeling. Let me try to elaborate on what has happened since I last updated this record.

The journey by vehicle out of the city and to this spot was uneventful, to say the least. Sgt. Janus met us at the proscribed spot, sporting very little baggage and acting as if he was merely setting out on a short jaunt around the park. I introduced him to Morrow and Weymouth and they barely gave him so much as a curious glance. I've learned that about the man; he can stand out when he wants to yet conversely maintain an extremely low profile when it suits him. We loaded the last of the gear in the truck and were on our way.

Spring is in full bloom throughout the countryside and the air is fresh and fragrant. I attempted to spur on conversation among my fellow travelers, but they would have none of it. Morrow in particular seemed sullen as we rode along, and Weymouth appeared content with just about anything that came his way – I find myself somewhat envious of him for that.

Morrow's dog, an animal of no specific breed, is a medium-sized thing and, for the most part, friendly. I am eager to observe it in the field, especially when we arrive at the cave, but until that point I can see the dog becoming terribly annoying, what with its periodic barking and almost-constant scratching. Morrow calls it Devil, a name I hope is not prophetic.

There was some discussion as to where we would stop along the road and make our insertion point in the forest, but I asserted my role as expedition leader and reminded everyone who was in charge. The spot at which I decided to make our base camp is approximately sixty miles southwest of Old Man's Cave – with luck, and providing we make good time on our hike, we should approach the cave in roughly two day's time.

Here, on the edge of the forest, I get a sense of how old it is. It is a massive thing, dense and shadowy, but also worthy of respect. Some might call the atmosphere here *ominous*; I label it *expectant*. It is a joy for me to attack such a case, finally free from seeking out spirits in crumbling old manor houses and drafty abbeys. If I had to spend one more minute in a decrepit little cemetery outside an equally-decrepit and disintegrating church with a fat, wheezing parson watching over my shoulder, I would surely have gone mad. The Ghost of Old Man's Cave should provide an ample respite from my usual work.

I must admit that Weymouth did an admirable job setting up the camp, under my supervision, and by nightfall we had fixed ourselves a fine meal and gathered around a cheerful fire. I hoped the mood would begin to change, but Janus had grown quiet since we stopped the truck and disembarked, and hadn't said a word since supper – if anything, he was acting as if the rest of us weren't even present. I spied him, well, testing the air, I suppose, and observing the forest around us. Many of our fellows hang much on the man's vaunted psychic sense, but so far it seems more a pretentious thing than a true ability or power. Still, there might be something to it.

A queer thing occurred after our meal, once we had cleared away the dishes and built the fire. Talk turned to our objective, which was entirely reasonable, and Weymouth asked me to elaborate on the case. As I began to elaborate on a few details for the big man, out of the corner of my eye I saw Janus turn and open the satchel I noticed he carried with him at all times. Then, I paused in my narrative as I saw that he had removed a small, wrapped object from his bag and placed it in his lap. Oh, I supposed Janus was merely attempting to join in the conversation, but to me it smacked of pulling the focus to himself. I asked what it was he had there.

Without saying a word, he slowly and with extreme care un-wrapped the object – to reveal a book. It was a small tome, but I im-mediately sized it up to be several hundred years old. Why the devil Janus would bring such an ancient volume out on a trip through the forest, knowing full well we would be "roughing it" for several days, is beyond me. I was of a mind to say just that when Morrow spoke up.

"That's a mighty old book, sir," he said. I would have liked to congratulate him on such an educated observation, but held my tongue in check.

"It is of an incredible vintage, yes," replied Janus. "I have owned it for many years; I think it may prove helpful on our sojourn."

Weymouth sat silently, staring at the book, and even the dog seemed mesmerized by it. Unable to hold my tongue, I asked the sergeant why he would risk such an obviously valuable volume here in the out-of-doors, among virtual strangers.

He turned to me and smiled slightly. "A good question, Blaylock. Here is my answer: it can only be opened in the 'out-of-doors," you see – in fact, only in an environment such as this." He gestured with one hand to the shadowy trees surrounding us and we all looked around. I myself was dubious of his claim but did not say so.

"This dates back at least a thousand years," he continued, hold-ing the book in both hands then. "It is the journal of a Viking sea captain, a most amazing account of his travels to foreign lands and what he encountered there."

I was conflicted, astounded that Janus would share such a price-less antiquity with us, but also sure that I had never heard of the Vikings making bound books…though I admit that such knowledge was not exactly in my realm of study. Janus smiled again and told me that the book had originally been personal writings on sheepskin and the like, and at some point of time later someone had bound the writings into book form.

"Here," he said. "Let me open it so that you might also marvel at its contents; this is only the third time I ever opened the book." Janus, ran his hand over the volume's strange-looking cover – was it leather of some sort? – and then to a small clasp or lock that held it shut. Loosening it, he opened the book to a page somewhere near its middle, a place that I could then see was marked by a silk ribbon. The mood shifted once he had opened the book, filling the circle with an odd sensation of…of what I cannot really say.

Janus began to read selected passages from what appeared to be a long narrative:

"We have come ashore and have made our way over this new and strange land for many days. Ahead of us is only forest, behind us the same. We are unsure of what drives us on and keeps us ever walking forward. The men are in good spirits, yes, but I feel as if the gods may not allow that for long.

"Now, we have come to a rocky place, full of cliffs and large stones and many carrion birds overhead. My scouts have returned and tell us that ahead lies a cave, a place where we might set ourselves down and that will shelter us from the coming storm. The men all feel that is a good thing, though I do not feel the gods' blessing upon it.

"The cave is large. It is surrounded by cliffs and a thickness of trees. This would be a very poor spot to have to defend, if we were at war. Here, we would be open to attack. I do not care for this place."

Janus paused and then looked up at each one of us in turn. "I see that you are all tired so I will jump ahead a little, and come to the pertinent passage. Listen closely to the words, my friends."

He turned a page, gingerly. I could see the writing was coarser, more hurried, in the section at which he had arrived.

"We have fled the area. Half my men are dead. The raging has taken them. The raging came upon us and stole the breath from our mouths and brought darkness. The cave is a monstrous place.

The gods have abandoned us, or perhaps all but one. The stones, the old, old stones rose up and wanted us to die. Many of us did and many of us will surely later die in spirit. We must make it back to the ship. There is nothing for us here. Less than nothing. Nothing but the raging."

Damn me, but I had fought hard to suppress a yawn throughout Janus' storytelling and ultimately lost the battle as he neared the end of his reading. He looked at me and cocked an eyebrow, but otherwise betrayed no emotion at my rudeness.

"I think you're saying that something at the cave killed them," remarked Morrow, after being quiet for a moment. "But it could have been anything – they could have eaten poisonous mushrooms, or some of them could have fallen off the cliffs. That's happened, and happened recently, in fact."

"Having eaten something that caused madness of a kind might explain the repeated reference to 'the raging,'" said Janus. "And I would tend to agree with you on your other theory, Mr. Morrow, but know this: I spent much time trying to decipher the term 'the raging' and I believe I now have a grasp on its meaning. These Vikings used it to identify not their own actions, but a very, very angry spirit...a ghost. A very old ghost."

Morrow considered this. I grew more fatigued by the second. Wanting very much to make this entry in my journal and then fall into a deep sleep, I made my farewells. Let Janus spend the rest of the night trying to impress the others, if that is what is important to him. I wanted to be fresh and rested for the days of walking that lie ahead.

MAY 1, 8:04 PM

Janus wants to turn back.

We have walked for most of the day and now the sun is setting, the shadows are growing deeper, Devil is nervous and Janus wants to turn back.

The day began well and I felt we were making good time, though

162

as we traveled further into the foothills the land grew more uneven and rocky. Still, we only stopped for brief rests and the air has been pleasant for most of the journey. Morrow has been an excellent guide, truly a stand-out. I was impressed with his knowledge of the terrain and the local flora, and he and his canine seemed to work as one being at times. Weymouth has been quiet, but perhaps that is for the best; he is not the most scintillating of conversationalists.

I tried then to engage the only other equal to myself in the group. Janus was open to chatting, at least at first, and I avoided topics related to our profession until I felt I had exhausted other subjects and turned to a few mentions of cases of mine. I had just finished telling him of a fascinating occurrence of unexplained stone moving in Anklesport when he smiled and turned to me.

"You've never actually seen a spirit, have you, Blaylock?" he asked.

My face burned a bit at that. "Well, no," I admitted. "We are not all so lucky to be world-recognized 'spirit-breakers,' Janus."

He chuckled a bit. "No need to be catty, my friend. I meant no insult by it. I only brought it up to reinforce, in a way, my reasons for coming on this investigation –"

He did not finish his statement and I had no time for rebuttal, for Morrow had called to us from many yards ahead. We had been following what he amusingly called a "trail," though if there was one visible I could not see it, and had now slowed. Something in Morrow's voice made me quicken my pace and catch up to him. Janus followed me, as well as Weymouth.

"What is it?" I inquired, seeing Morrow down upon one knee and clearing some dead leaves off what looked like a stone. His dog paced around, circling its master.

"This," said our guide, and pointed at the stone. I could see nothing, or at least nothing he should be concerned about. I told him I didn't understand and that if it was fine with him I thought we should continue on our way. Morrow looked up at me with an odd expression on his face and then at Janus.

"This shouldn't be here," he said, plainly.

Before I could ask him to explain such a cryptic and dramatic statement, Janus knelt down and touched the stone. Then, drawing something out from his satchel, he passed the object over the stone. "A petroglyph," he announced and then I could see it – a small sigil etched into the rock and as ancient-looking as the day was long.

"Yep," replied Morrow. "I'm the only one who knows it's here. Or, rather, where it should be."

The device Janus had manifested was a simple arrangement, a string with a small weight tied to one end that he hung down over a small, grey tablet. On the tablet were symbols and letters; a Franwellian Pointer, or, in some circles, now known as a Janus Pointer.

Janus stood and deposited the tool back in his bag. It's a fascinating device, with actual, sound principals behind it and quite the rage now among our lot. I own one myself, but must admit that I have never really mastered its use and left it at home.

"The glyph is of incredible vintage, my friend," Janus noted. "But why should it concern you so?"

"As I said, it doesn't belong here. We shouldn't have come up on it for another half-day's travel. In fact, looking around now, this all looks mighty queer."

Well, to hear our guide, the only man recommended to me for the job, make such a pronouncement was nothing short of disquieting. I was very sure he hadn't been hitting the bottle while we walked, so it was a very disturbing comment. I would have liked to inquire further as to his reasoning behind his statements, but Morrow suddenly took off at a brisk pace and before I knew it had scaled a small rise not more than fifty feet or so from the stone. He stood on the rise and looked beyond it, shaking his head.

Janus called out to him, asked him to come back. Morrow shrugged and did so. Janus then pointed at Devil. "Look," he said.

The canine was frozen in place. It was the most astounding thing; the dog had taken a position of, well, pointing, I presume, and had seemingly become stuck. Morrow shook his head again and muttered to himself. Janus motioned for us to remain where we were and stalked up to the rise himself, slowly and deliberately. When he drew near to the upward slope of the ground, he reached into his pocket and drew out another small object. This one I could not see as it was small enough to be almost completely covered by his hand. Then, slowly and with some apparent slight physical impediment, he topped the rise and held up his hand with the object in it.

Janus stood on the rise for almost a full minute, slightly turning one way and then the other. Satisfied, apparently, he withdrew the object and, placing it back into his pocket, he returned to us.

"We must leave," he said, solemnly. "We must turn around and head back to our base camp."

I protested most strongly. "Janus! What do you mean by that? I am the leader of this expedition and head investigator – it will be me who says if we are to abort the mission. And what is that object you used up there? Why do you say we must return?"

"Blaylock, a word in private, please," he said, and drew me off to one side. "See here, my young friend; we are in danger. I cannot state that more plainly. Morrow is correct when he says we are not where we should be. In fact, we are far closer to the cave than either he or myself thought possible after only walking a single day. There is some…influence at work here, but of what nature I am unsure. You see that rise there? That is its boundary. Past that, we would be in its range, and that is not a place where we would want to be. I have glimpsed a terrible presence beyond it – human, but quite terrible.

"We must turn around, if you value your life and the lives of everyone else present."

Here I now sit, pondering those words and replaying them in my mind until they make little sense to me. I managed to convince the poor man that we should take a brief rest and consider all of our options, not wanting to excite him further. Then, after we had broken out a few provisions, I then suggested we make camp as it was getting to be much too late to start walking back to the road. He acceded to my wishes and here we are for the night, at the edge of the rise – Janus' so-called "boundary."

Tomorrow morning, I will decide what is that we shall do. Tonight, I am remembering the sage advice of Calliope.

MAY 2, 4:27 AM

Things have gone poorly. Let me try to explain, though it is hard to write in the darkness with only a flashlight for illumination.

Three hours ago, I decided not to wait until sunrise to make my decision but rose from my tent and, gathering up Morrow, I struck out on my own. Our rough-hewn guide protested at first, issuing forth with some sort of misguided loyalty to Sgt. Janus, yet I reminded him who was paying his way – he agreed then to lead me to the cave. At the time, it seemed like the perfectly logical and high-minded thing to do, but now I regret my actions. The whole investigation has come crashing down around me.

My respect for Janus is still present, and I look over at him now and feel gratitude towards him, but he is of an infuriating mien. Still...

Morrow and I made headway through the forest and I was astounded at his ability to see his way in piercing the utter darkness. It was troubling, though, when he muttered to himself that the distances felt wrong and that he very likely had no real idea of what we were heading into. As we traveled, I felt the forest begin to press in on me and a touch of claustrophobia crept into my awareness. I will not go so far as to say that the trees were, well, *alive*, but there was some tangible force surrounding us that seemed to follow Morrow and myself for miles. I remember hoping that day would break soon and the darkness would recede, as I had no real wish to arrive at the site in darkness. It would not be conducive to my investigation.

I also remember too well Morrow's terse exclamation of profanity when we came to the edge of a cliff and nearly over it. When I had re-gathered my wits I told him to be quiet and to explain why it was that he was so surprised at our location – was he not the guide? He turned to me with an expression of panic mingled with disgust. He did not know what to make of it, he said...we were already at the cave.

Here is the scene as it lay before me: At the edge of the cliff, I looked out into an immense gorge or depression or natural bowl in the earth. Ringed with trees, it reminded me of a giant set of hands cupped together – it had to have been the very sight the Vikings in Janus' book witnessed when they first approached the area. It was dark, oh so very dark down in the depression, but I hauled out my pair of field glasses anyway and peered through them. I searched in vain for several minutes to discern the cave, then heard heavy breathing in my ear. Morrow's mutt. I cursed at it and it stepped back.

For some reason, at that moment, I felt an odd pang of regret that Janus and I had been forced to go separate ways and that he was not there to share in the experience of being in the cave's vicinity. Then, I spotted it – a craggy outcropping of rock that formed a kind of ersatz doorway or archway and inside it the deepest, darkest, most Stygian black: Old Man's Cave.

I tried to sort out my feelings at that moment but decided to suppress them all and approach the task at hand with a clinical, scientific mind; this was an investigation, and I had work to do. Whispering, I told Morrow to begin to set up the tripod and camera and we would then wait for the sun to begin to rise for a round of documentary photography.

Then, through my field glasses, I saw something at the mouth of the cave.

It seemed to – no, it *did* appear out of nothing. Can that be correct? One moment, there was simply blackness, then a figure was there, the figure of a man or something man-like. It formed out of the very air, I swear it, like the very shadows of the cave broke off a piece of themselves and molded a man like a sculptor works clay. But, this was something intangible – I could see the edges of the rocky cave opening through it! It wavered in the air, blobby yet holding the vague shape of man, becoming more *real*, in a way, by the second. *The thing was entering our plane of existence.* I wiped and rubbed at my eyes; the figure defied them. If this was not our spirit, the very ghost of the cave, then I did not know what it was.

Devil growled and pawed at the ground. I had a question that needed to be answered: "Can a ghost kill?" Without turning my head, I told Morrow to release his canine.

I thought the man might strike me, so apparently irate was he at the thought. I was about to order him to do as I said, when,

167

through the glasses, I saw the form at the mouth of the cave completely disappear.

Then, chaos.

Let me try to piece this together – my hand is quaking as I write and the flashlight is failing. Oh, dear Lord, let me get this down…I heard Morrow's voice catch and crack. He was choking. Devil screamed, a horrible, horrible sound. When I turned around I saw…I saw…what did I see? What did I see? Morrow's feet off the ground – both of them. Choking, gasping sounds, punctuating the darkness. Cold, oh so cold! Something catching the moonlight, struggling with Morrow – no, not the moonlight – it was generating its own light, a cold, dead light. The spirit! The spirit – it was upon us! The wretched thing – what else could it have been? The thing had seen us and then it was gone and then it was on the cliff with us and it had Morrow…and his head falling back and…and his throat…God, his throat was collapsing…his entire neck caving in… the dog snarling and clawing…

Can a ghost kill? Yes, yes; a ghost can kill.

MAY 2, 4:38 AM

I am back. I will write out the rest. The thing killed Morrow. Then, Janus appeared.

One moment I had prepared for the worst and the next, the sergeant was there and yelling in a deep voice, but not at me. At the ghost. He was yelling something at the ghost. And Janus was waving something at it.

The unearthly thing vanished. With a sucking of the air, it was gone. I realized I was still lying on my stomach at the edge of the cliff when Janus reached down and, calling my name, grabbed me and pulled me up.

"We must *go*, Blaylock," he said. Yes, that is what he said. And we went.

We shuffled along for approximately twenty yards and when we had reached a small clearing, we stopped. I asked him – how did I ever find my voice? – what we were doing, but he ignored me. Janus was drawing in the dirt and leaves. He sketched out a circle, perhaps fifteen feet in diameter, and told me to step inside of it. Something of my old self then manifested, brought about by Janus' actions, and I made my protest.

"See here, Janus," I began. "I know what you are doing now. You can't believe for a single moment that this *circle* will help us! We need to move away from this spot! And quickly! Why would you waste your – our! – time with this empty gesture? There is absolutely no proof, no documentation, that these *circles* work! *We are in dire peril, man!*"

He stepped up to me and bodily placed me in the circle. He then beckoned the dog and once it had joined us he began waving something around the circle and mumbling under his breath.

"There," he said, finally. "That may hold. Do not leave this circle, under *any* circumstances, Blaylock. Do I make myself clear? It is our only real chance to make it out of this alive."

Drained almost completely of energy, I found I had little tongue left in me. But I did ask him what it was that he had been waving about; Janus extended his hand and there in his palm lay a small, dark disk. This was the object I had seen him use the day before at the "boundary" of this spirit's domain. He cautioned me not to touch it; I asked him what it was, exactly.

"There is no real name for it," he said. "It is the only one that I know of – if there are others, I am not aware of their existence. As to why I warn against touching it, that is because no man, no living creature, may look at its face."

"But why?" I asked him. "Why would that be, Janus? This smacks of thaumaturgy – medicine shows and the like. Surely this is not science…what is on its face?"

Despite the circumstances, despite the fact that we were sitting in an occult circle in the middle of an immense forest with some sort of murderous, vengeful entity somewhere in the vicinity, Janus smiled.

"Well…I do not know," he replied. "Perhaps nothing. Nothing at all."

I stared at him. "Then," I said. "If that is so, why does it seem to...to route this spirit? How does it work?"

Janus looked at me, really looked at me. "I do not know that either. Perhaps it only works because I believe it will."

That was several minutes ago. Janus now sits off to one side of me; I believe he may be meditating. Devil sits next to him and occasionally looks over at me as I write. I am calm now. I have gained a composure that is once again allowing me to think and to think clearly. This is a survivable situation; of that I am now certain. The spirit has not returned. I have begun to ponder the events of the past few hours and have come to the conclusion that on many aspects I may be confused. Yes, I was not thinking clearly – now I am. This allows me to make these notes, of which I am very thankful.

The sun will be coming up before long and we shall return to our camp. From there, I will lay out my new plan to Janus and Weymouth, a plan that will allow us to continue the investigation and complete the mission. I admit that I was a bit hasty before and went off somewhat half-cocked, but with the new day comes new clarity and new avenues of possibility. I will concede to Janus on a few salient points and in doing so perhaps we can come to an agreement as to how we shall proceed.

It is so very dark still. I have noticed that there are no signs or sounds of insects or other creatures...but I seem to be hearing something now. Dogs? There is the sound of what I believe to be dogs, off in the distance. I looked over at Devil, forgetting myself for a moment, but he is here with us, in the circle. Neither he nor Janus seems to notice the howling. This damnable darkness! My light is almost completely gone...

MAY 8, 7:44 AM

My friend is gone. Completely, utterly gone.

Every explanation for this situation I can conjure seems hollow and empty. I am a sham, and I have lost something the world most desperately needs. I lay here in my bed, near to a week after the denouement of that wretched day and I strain to compose my thoughts. To write this is to try and conjure up those horrific moments – and it is a painful thing, indeed.

The ghost came upon us again, all anger and violence. It swept up and over us and Janus yelled to me that the circle he had erected would protect us. It did *seem* to...to hold back the thing that very clearly wanted to get inside. I was able to get a better look at the spirit and could see it was very large, and though it looked to be intangible it was also able to manipulate and displace the ground and foliage around it. Incredible.

Then, I broke the circle. Not Janus, not the dog, but me.

When the thing swelled up to engulf us, I forgot myself and, as humans have done for tens of thousands of years, I instinctively moved into a defensive mode. I had spied a hefty branch laying on the ground not more than three feet from us earlier and, when I felt threatened, I reacted without thinking. I grabbed for the branch. The branch was outside Janus' circle. The circle I had already impugned. And I broke it.

Oh, Blaylock – you poor, sad fool...

The thing was upon Janus in an instant. He pushed me out of the way, but, if it knew I was even present, it gave no notice – it clearly wanted Janus. Perhaps it felt he was its chief tormentor, its prime enemy. But, what was it? *Who* was it? If it had ever even been anyone at all...if it was ever truly alive. But, at least I do not sense that it was an infernal beast; I feel as if it were the ghost of someone long, long dead.

Janus struggled mightily with it, heroically. He...he waved with his hand for me to run away, but I was frozen in place, damn me. I could do nothing but watch in terror and horror at the impossible sight before me. My friend wielded his disc, his improbable sigil, and again and again the thing rushed at him. Janus then shouted to *me* to close the circle.

His voice tore through me, all pain and torment, but commanding; it broke me from my stunned reverie and my mind raced to complete the task.

But how? There was a tremendous crushing rush of air around us that whipped at me and slowed my actions. Repair the circle? Me? Good Lord! I had made it my habit to eschew such things as the emptiest of promises – and Janus was screaming at *me* to close the circle of protection he had made.

The air beat at me like a thousand hammers – good Lord! I could scarcely breathe or see! But, from somewhere deep inside my frame, from the depths of my training, I dredged up a memory, a passage or two I had once read from some ancient tome and then as quickly discarded. I spit on my hands – no easy chore at that moment – took hold of the branch I had been reaching for, spit once more on the ground at my feet and recited an arcane phrase while re-connecting the circle. Re-connecting our defense.

The world then collapsed on me. The moment I'd completed the circle, the air was simply *absent*. A mighty vacuum formed and then exploded with resounding impact. I saw…I saw…what did I see? Did I only…feel it in my body? The spirit…the great, attacking spirit broke up, broke up into a multitude of other beings…then Janus…oh, I saw things. Heard things. *Voices.* Great and powerful voices, in many languages, most of them queer to me. Faces sprang at me, one after another, as if someone was throwing a deck of cards at me, one by one. Faces of death and of pain. Oh, Lord…

Janus was yelling. His voice…I could hear it. Then, suddenly, silence.

Blackness. All was dark. No air…no air to breathe.

I awoke an hour later. Maybe a bit more. Devil looked down at me, sitting quietly and attentively by my side. But no Sgt. Janus. No body. No vengeful ghost. Nothing. As if they never existed.

I cannot write any more today.

MAY 9, 11:16 AM

It has been one full week since those horrific events, and for myself, they remain an open wound. Let this record show that I freely admit my guilt in this matter and take full responsibility. A great man has been cut down and all I can think now is that I wish it had been me, for I have heard people speak of hubris and now know exactly what they mean.

Sgt. Roman Janus was a great man; I see that now. Or, rather, I am reminded of that now. I have always known that, but had simply forgotten. I said long ago, as the "Spirit-Breaker" he was an idol of mine and that is still true. Once I am well and able to move about again, I will…will tell the world of the man's great deeds, of his accomplishments and triumphs. He only wished to help others. That is all he ever set out to do, to come to the aid of those who faced the unknown, the supernatural and feared it. Janus asked little for himself and he gave much. He was selfless, as selfless as a man could be…what was it that he himself wrote in his own *Theosophy of Eternity*? "Though we witness the world beyond death, we must strive to make our lives the final statement."

I feel as if it is of vast importance to make a record of these events. People will need to know of the successful conclusion of my expedition. My question has been answered, all too well. At the precise moment that Weymouth found me on that lonely spot and began to help me back to civilization, I felt guilt drape over me like a cloak. Oh, I have robbed the world of much and, in doing so, I will be haunted to the end of my days.

But perhaps, just perhaps, if not consolation I may still find answers.

MAY 12, 5:55 PM

I have just returned from the site. There is no indication, no trace, no sign of Janus' body nor of the spirit that brought him down. Even the circle is gone. I cannot explain it. I know that it all happened, but…

The weight of each day, each hour and minute we spent there in that forsaken wood is lade upon me.

Until I can fathom it, this must remain an unfinished record.

DEVELOPERS DISCOVER "SPIRIT-BREAKER" PAPERS

The former *Mount Airy Eagle* building was recently purchased by Trans-Global Media Partners and cleared for demolition. Documents dating back to the mid-1800s were discovered in the basement of the building. Among the papers was a curious document that appears to be a transcript of an interview by an *Eagle* writer with Sgt. Roman Janus, the infamous Spirit-Breaker of the early 20th century. The date of the interview is unknown.

The *Eagle* ran a regular column during that period called "The Professional Corner," a series of interviews with people representing various professions, in an effort to illuminate business concerns and other related interests. The column featured two writers, Cortland Smith and Norman Prapps, but it remains unclear which writer conducted the interview. For reasons that cannot be determined, the interview was never published. However, based on the typical format of the column, it would have likely been edited into a prose format prior to publication, rather than the question-and-answer format seen here.

The interview offers a rare and somewhat candid perspective on Roman Janus, and we are happy to present it to you.

Interviewer: Please state your name and profession.

Janus: I am Sgt. Roman E. Janus, Spirit-Breaker.

Interviewer: Could you be more precise, sir, in your profession?

Janus: Certainly. I aid those who are troubled by the supernatural.

Interviewer. Quite. And what forms may the 'supernatural' assume to trouble people?

Janus: Oh, well, far too many, to be sure. I generally weigh in on matters of hauntings and other such spectral or near-spectral visitations, but I also have been known to consult and take a more direct hand in possessions, both human and inanimate objects. I rarely turn anyone away who comes to me with a worrisome problem of a psychical nature.

Interviewer: Would you say that there are many people you meet in your trade who do not believe in the supernatural or ghosts?

Janus: Yes, and I very much sympathize with them. The etheric world has yet to fully capture the attention and belief of the general populace, and, if I might say so, I almost envy them that ignorance. It is not an easy life, that of a Spirit-Breaker, and there are days when I would just as soon pick up a good book and a nice brandy than banish another arduous spirit.

Interviewer: You say 'has yet to fully capture' – do you mean, sir that...well, that seems to indicate something rather ominous on the horizon for mankind.

Janus: I humbly apologize if I alarmed you. What I mean to say is that the connection between the waking world and the spirit plane has grown closer over the past several hundred years and will continue to do so, but it will be several more centuries before any possibility of full juxtaposition. You and I shall be long into dust by then. Have no fear.

Interview: Well, then, how do you 'break' these spirits? Do you utilize more than one way of interjecting yourself into these...these 'situations'?

Janus: Generally, it's a matter of spotting the connection point and analyzing its nature. From there I choose from several different, ah, surgical strikes to sever the ties between the spirits and the living. And not all of them are of a violent bent. Sometimes, the kid glove is just as effective as the saber. The intention is to send the dead on their proper way, along the path that was always meant for them. For the most part, the spirits are not entirely responsible for their earthly imprisonment or the pain and suffering that often comes along with it. Such souls need to be shown the door with dignity and decorum.

Interview: But there are those spirits that have been, shall we say, reluctant to heed your direction?

Janus: Yes. Rather a lot, really. Those cases I must approach more forcefully, and, yes, even violently. It is a strange business sometimes.

Interview: I should say so. It boggles the mind. Why would

such an injustice exist? It seems a poor way to run a universe, if the Almighty will forgive me for saying so.

Janus: More than a few people have remarked upon that to me, and I tell them all the same thing: I cannot speak for the Deity and His purposes and His reasoning. I am but His humble servant and operate as I see fit to set the system right when it goes wrong.

Interviewer: Then you are a religious man, sir?

Janus: Well, what is religion, really? A system, like many others, of course, beset by rules and regulations, but with the object of bringing peace and happiness under our Lord here on Earth. I do not subscribe to any organized church or services, but practice a religion of one. Some may not see it as a religion, but again I ask you: what is a religion?

Interviewer: We would not presume to debate you on that score, so let us move on. You have published several books on the subject of the supernatural and spiritualism, each one of them entirely unlike any other authors' volumes on the like. Are you working on anything at the moment? Will we be seeing your memoirs before long?

Janus: Memoirs are for the dead, or the near-dead. If I should ever be moved to write such a book or set of books, I will wait until after I am long departed. For the here and now, I am currently toiling on a volume I shall title *The Ghost of Sumatra*, which will detail a most fascinating case, one of the most unique of my career to date. When it will be finished, I cannot say, for there are certain aspects of the case that continue to this day.

Interviewer: Sgt. Janus, you run your operation with no partners, no employees, and if I am not mistaken, you are not a married man. Is there anyone in your life at this time, a special someone, someone who perhaps understands your profession and could possibly even aid you in it?

Janus: Ah, look at the time. I'm afraid this has taken a bit longer than I expected. Thank you very much for having me and please send me a note when the article will be published. I will look forward to it. Good day, sir.

Interviewer: And to you, sir. A very good day. Thank you.

GIVING THE GHOST-HUNTER
A GHOST OF CHANCE

If you didn't care much for the stories in this collection, you could blame Alan Moore. If you, in fact, liked the stories, you may possibly owe him a small note of thanks.

You see, it was the infamous comic scribe himself who set me down the labyrinthine path that led to the creation of Sgt. Roman Janus and the world he haunts. No, I don't know Moore personally, but I know his work, and one story in particular opened up a brave new world of literary inspirations for me: *The League of Extraordinary Gentlemen*.

After devouring the first volume of Moore's *League* back in 1999, I realized I knew precious little of the characters in the great work other than their fame in the greater world of film apart from their literary origins. My consumption of the original novels that spawned The League's members soon followed and likewise for the second volume of Moore's landmark series. Afterwards, I felt more well-rounded, in a literary sense. When news of Volume Three finally rolled around, I heard about the "new" characters involved, including one "Carnacki." Intrigued, I began searching for his tales.

The original Carnacki stories by author William Hope Hodgson are a real trick-or-treat for ghost story aficionados. I bought the 2006 Wordsworth edition of *The Casebook of Carnacki the Ghost Finder*, which includes all nine of Hodgson's tales of the character, and read one story a night for nine spooky evenings. I was hooked; written from 1910 to 1913, the stories are both incredibly atmospheric and engaging. Our Hero is an investigator of occult occurrences who uses both arcane instruments and modern devices to root out ghost hoaxers and real specters alike, all the while comporting himself as a true Edwardian gentlemen and a kind of successor to Sherlock Holmes – at least in the spook department.

Carnacki wasn't the first of this type of early 20th century character that I'd read; the first volume of Moore's *League* got me hooked on Sax Rohmer's Fu Manchu novels, which in turn led me to the author's Dream Detective stories. But it was Carnacki who first put the germ of an idea to write my own such tales in my fevered, haunted brain. Once *The League of Extraordinary Gentlemen Century: 1910* came out in 2009 and revealed an entire gentlemen's club populated by a witch's coven of Edwardian occult characters, I knew the die was cast and my fate was sealed; Sgt. Janus began to take free-floating form.

I then gobbled up similar tales by Alice and Claude Askew, M.P. Shiel, M. Somerset Maugham, Manly Wade Wellman, Algernon Blackwood and others. They all helped to cement what I actually hoped to accomplish with my own character. I knew I wanted to echo Hodgson and the others, but not strictly copy them. I wanted to honor the entire Edwardian occult investigator genre, but not ape it. Again, Carnacki led the way and Sgt. Janus continued to gestate as my own ode to the "proto-pulp" heroes of the early 1900s.

There were three elements in general with which I wanted to endow my character: a unique landscape, interesting clients and real ghosts to bust – no hoaxes. The first would involve a literary setting that has always intrigued me: a "magic" house. It just so happened that one of my most favorite books of all time, James Stoddard's 1998 novel *The High House*, was inspired by the works of Hodgson, so the literary web was already firmly in play. In Stoddard's world, the High House is a mansion that literally goes on forever and encompasses a multitude of realms and peoples; my own smaller version, Janus House, grew out of that idea. Though I knew many scenes would be set in the house's myriad rooms, I also wanted my hero to be ambulatory in the outside world, unlike another of my idols, Rex Stout's Nero Wolfe. So Janus would go wherever spirits vexed innocent people. That would lead to interesting clients, hope-fully, and cover my second point.

As for my ban against "Scooby Doo" endings – you know the type, where the mask comes off and the very corporeal villain stands revealed – I had no desire to tease anyone with the question of whether my ghosts were real, in the ectoplasmic sense. Janus would never involve himself with such cases; he knows a real spirit when he senses one…and when it needs breaking.

Side note: I have a very tangible love-hate relationship with the subject of ghosts and hauntings. Not fully a believer nor a skeptic, I have for all my life been interested in such things…and scared of them, too. It's incredibly interesting to me how one can consciously discuss the possibility of the non-existence of ghosts yet at the same time feel that niggling trill of fright in the most primitive part of the human brain. Some days I laugh at the subject, other nights I'm cowering under the bed because one of those ghost hunters pro-grams on cable scares the bejeeburs out of me.

So, I had my investigator, his profession, his headquarters and his clientele. All I needed were his stories. Some of them came to me immediately, whole cloth; others grew organically as I wrote, drawn from events "as they happened." It was a fun process as I chal-lenged myself throughout the period in which I wrote these eight tales…and also tried to scare myself from time to time. And the linking motif that threads its way through all the stories also came about as I wrote, a way to grow the universe I was creating.

As I was pondering all the mischief Janus could get himself into, I began to think about the narrative style I wanted to employ. The set-up in these types of stories usually involved the hero sit-ting around regaling someone else – an assistant or even a group of neighborhood youths – with his cases, but I wanted something… different. Somehow, in some way, I stumbled across the idea of the sergeant's clients each telling their own stories, instead of the man himself or a Dr. Watson-type of character. This would allow me to come at the stories from many points of view and to invoke many kinds of "voices" in doing so. I looked around and even asked a few knowledgeable people, and it seemed, on the surface, to be a relatively unique device. Satisfied with the foundations I'd laid, I tucked into the stories...

"The Portobello Cetacean" was conceived as an introduction to Sgt. Janus' world, a kind of primer on what the reader could expect from his cases. The woman who comes to the Spirit-Breaker for help would be a bit of an anomaly for her time – driving her own automobile for jaunts outside the city and conferring with strange men – but I grew to admire her pluck and sympathize with her plight. This story also owes a tiny debt to Angela Lansbury.

The central figure of "A Bad Business" reared his bad attitude as a way for me to counterpoint the first story; whereas the woman therein became fond of Janus and interested in his work, the business owner in this second tale is, as we say, not a fan. This came out to be one of my most favorite of the stories in the book; its dramatic finale is etched very visually in my mind. I do sincerely hope, though, the story doesn't conjure up too many bad memories of any one particular "boss from hell" for anyone.

Ghosts don't always have to haunt houses and castles and whatnot, I figured, so what about something smaller, like a trunk? "This Unbroken Lock" allowed me to set a haunted bit of furniture on a stage, in front of an audience, and watch what popped out. I really enjoyed the challenge of writing the voice of a less, shall we say, uneducated person than the previous two stories' protagonists. Dam is a character I'd love to return to some day and see what he's up to; he has a job of which I myself am envious. Ahh, to be around all those books...

"Lydia's Lover" begins what I think of as "the story within the stories" found in this book. It came from a desire to once again utilize a female narrator and to write a kind of romance story. It was also during the writing of this tale that I began to realize that I wanted something more than "just" a collection of loose knit stories about an Edwardian occult investigator, but rather something more like a series of tales that equal one greater narrative. So Lydia and her late lover entered Janus' world and threw a monkey wrench into his neatly ordered life. Maybe I'm just a cruel, cruel man, but I think – or at least hope – it spiced things up all the more for my Spirit-Breaker.

Another of my personal favorites among the stories is "The Corkworth Fortune." I mean, where else can a writer have the wonderful opportunity to get into the head of such a flamboyant ne'er-do-well like Holden Muir? I tried like the dickens to build the story in such a way as to obscure the true identity of the murderer…not sure if I succeeded, but boy did I enjoy the attempt. And that tunnel thing there in the Room of Cabinets? Brrr…

"Sculpted Velvet" also grew out of a desire to once again do something a bit different with the narrator. After writing five previous tales with clients full of emotions and opinions, it was a nice change of pace – and a challenge – to think like a seemingly-emotionless policeman. By the way, you've probably heard of, or experienced for yourself, that phenomenon of a fictional character "telling" its creator what it wants to do, rather than the other way around. I wasn't sure I ever really believed such accounts when I'd come across them, but, so help me, that's what happened to me as I wrote this tale. Officer McPeek surprised me when he clocked poor Janus on the noggin – that wasn't what I intended. But what do I know? I'm only the writer…and it did make sense within the action.

Remember when I said that I tried to scare myself while I wrote? "When the Rain Comes" is the result of a concerted effort on my part to give myself the creeping creeps. I found that I felt more creative and "in the story" if I wrote only at night, in a room completely by myself and with only one small source of light. It worked, for the most part, as I found myself taking more and more breaks to get up and remove myself to a more well-lit room. Some of the "visitations" herein are what I imagine to be some of the more spooky ways that ghosts could approach us the living, and one scene in particular actually happened to me as a child. Or so I believe. It also helped that it rained for days on end as I wrote this tale – true story.

And so we come to "The Unfinished Record." It will be very, very interesting to me to hear the reaction to this story, and I sincerely hope readers will find a way to let me know what they think of it. Somewhere in the middle of writing the stories, I began to think about how I wanted to end the book and what I wanted to leave the reader with. Assuming I've done my job and done it well, I hope readers will become, to some degree, attached to Roman Janus. He remains a kind of enigma, yes, and that's by design, but I wanted him to also be an honorable figure and a man whom people could trust and rely upon. His world is a dangerous one; there's no getting around that, but perhaps there also exists within it hope, for with hope Sgt. Janus may someday and in some strange way return. There are clues to this, possibilities, which are peppered throughout this story and in some of the others. Who knows what may happen next? It may all depend on *you*.

I would like to gratefully acknowledge a few incredibly important people who aided me in the crafting of this novel: James Stoddard and Armando Rivera for encouragement at an early and crucial stage; Joe Berenato for a precious set of extra eyes, and helpful comments; Jeff Hayes for the cover that sparked a thousand wows in me; Ron Fortier of Airship 27, publisher of the prior edition of this book for his steadfast believe in the project and his eternal patience; and John Bruening, the better half of Flinch Books, for wisdom and wordsmithing when I fell short at times on both.

ALSO AVAILABLE FROM

FLINCH!
B O O K S

SOMETHING STRANGE IS GOING ON:
NEW TALES FROM THE FLETCHER
HANKS UNIVERSE
Ten new stories spotlighting characters
originally conceived by one of the most
offbeat creators from the Golden Age of
comics.

"...a tribute to the man's twisted, warped
genius."
–The British Fantasy Society

BIG TOP TALES:
SIX NEW TALES OF CIRCUS
ADVENTURE
Follow the Henderson & Ross Royal Circus
on a coast-to-coast journey of mystery,
mayhem and murder during its 1956
summer season.

"...a stellar collection...Highly
recommended."
–Ron Fortier, Pulp Fiction Reviews

Available on
AMAZON.COM
and
BARNESANDNOBLE.COM

ALSO AVAILABLE FROM

FLINCH! BOOKS

***RESTLESS:
AN ANTHOLOGY OF MUMMY
HORROR***
Six stories chronicling the ancient dead
from around the globe who reemerge from
the tomb to mete out a dark vengeance and
balance the eternal scales.

"If you love old-fashioned horror…dim the
lights and sit down for an evening of reading
pleasure."
–Ron Fortier, Pulp Fiction Reviews

***QUEST FOR THE SPACE GODS:
THE CHRONICLES OF
CONRAD VON HONIG***
This world-renowned yet controversial
author will search every inch of the globe
to find the truth about ancient aliens
…or die trying.

"If you thrilled at the notion of ancient
astronauts as a kid of the '70s, von Honig's
travels will have you longing once more
for an interstellar brotherhood to which
humanity might one day aspire."
–Amazon Review

Available on
AMAZON.COM
and
BARNESANDNOBLE.COM

Made in the USA
Monee, IL
05 August 2021